C463914242

T0109626

THE GREEK'S NINE-MONTH SURPRISE

BY

JENNIFER FAYE

First published in Great Britain 2016
By Mills & Boon, an imprint of HarperCollins*Publishers*
1 London Bridge Street, London, SE1 9GF

Large Print edition 2016

© 2016 Jennifer F. Stroka

ISBN: 978-0-263-26246-9

Our policy is to use papers that are natural, renewable
and recyclable products and made from wood grown
in sustainable forests. The logging and manufacturing
processes conform to the legal environmental regulations
of the country of origin.

Printed and bound in Great Britain
by CPI Antony Rowe, Chippenham, Wiltshire

For Lois.
To an amazing lady who always makes me smile.
Thanks for your support.

PROLOGUE

THE WEDDING BOUQUET tumbled through the air.

The breath caught in Sofia Moore's throat as she watched the flowers sail end over end. They were headed her way. She raised her hands high in the air. With a firm grasp on the bouquet, she smiled triumphantly, thankful her friend had chosen flowers that didn't bother her allergies. Sofia lowered her arms, taking a moment to admire the beautiful white lilies and the delicate blue orchids.

As a round of applause went up, she lifted her head. Her gaze immediately met a set of piercing blue-gray eyes. Only one person had such mesmerizing eyes. Niko Stravos.

Her heart pounded in her chest. He quickly averted his gaze, but the connection had been long enough for her stomach to quiver with excitement. He liked her. Of that she was certain.

In turn, she was drawn to him like a honeybee to a sun-warmed daisy. How could she not be? He was drop-dead gorgeous in the tall, dark and dreamy sort of way. But there was something more—something she couldn't quite put her finger on.

She moved to where he was standing. His stance was a bit stiff, and a frown marred his handsome face. What had caused him to look so uncomfortable? Just moments ago, they'd been enjoying their time together. Their conversation had been light and entertaining. She wasn't ready for it to end.

"Care to dance again?" She hoped to cajole him back into a good mood.

Niko's hesitant gaze zeroed in on the bouquet before returning to her face. "Perhaps we should rest. Aren't you tired?"

"Tired? Not a chance. I love weddings." This was the first time since she'd called off her engagement that she'd truly enjoyed herself. She didn't want this magical evening to end. "Don't you?"

"What?" Lines creased between his dark brows.

"Don't you enjoy weddings?"

His gaze moved to the colorful lilies again. "Not so much. I'm usually too busy at the office to attend them."

"In that case, you should make the most of the occasion. I'm sure Kyra's glad you made an exception today." She noticed how his attention kept straying back to the flowers. She turned and placed the arrangement on the bridal table. But still the pensive look on his face remained. "I love this song. Let's go dance."

He shook his head. "I don't think so."

"But why?"

He glanced around as though trying to avoid her pointed stare. "You should dance with someone else. I...I don't want to take up your entire evening. I should go."

"But we were having fun. Don't say goodbye. Not yet." She needed this—she needed to feel alive again after beating herself up for letting herself stay in a dead-end relationship for too long. "Please."

Niko hesitated. Then he held out his arm to her. "Shall we?"

A smile pulled at her lips. "I thought you'd never ask."

He escorted her onto the crowded dance floor that had been erected on the beach of the Blue Tide Resort beneath a giant tent supported by white columns. Everyone around them was smiling and laughing. The tables were adorned with white linens, floral centerpieces and votive candles. It was so easy to get swept up in the joyful celebration of her best friend's wedding.

A smile lifted the corners of his mouth. "You are unlike anyone I've ever known. I never know what to expect from you."

"I like to keep you guessing." She stepped into his very capable arms.

"You enjoy being different, don't you?"

"Yes." There was no hesitation in her response. None whatsoever. "I tried living up to someone's expectations. I turned myself inside out, and it still wasn't enough. In fact, it was an utter disaster. Since then, I've decided to march to my own drum."

"And how's that working for you?"

"Quite well." After all, she was dancing the night away with the most eligible bachelor at this wedding. "Quite well indeed. You should try it."

His eyes widened. "And what makes you think I don't march to my own drum?"

"Just a feeling."

He struck her as the conservative type, from his restrained emotions to his proper hold on her as they danced; not standing too close and his hands always remained in a respectable place. But then there was his longer, wavy dark hair. And the way he stared at her when he didn't think she noticed. Perhaps there was an impulsive side to him just longing to get out. She relished the idea.

Wanting to push him out of his safety zone, she moved closer to him. Her curves brushed up against his muscular chest. Immediately he sucked in a deep breath as his body stiffened.

"Relax," she murmured, feeling exceedingly daring. Perhaps it was the dim lighting. Or maybe it was the sparkling wine. Whatever it was, she decided not to fight it. She was having too much fun. "Don't worry—I won't bite."

A deep, rich chuckle rumbled from his chest. They began to move to the music again. He leaned in close—real close. His breath lightly brushed over her neck, sending goose bumps down her arms. "Why do I get the feeling you're trying to take advantage of me?"

She swallowed hard, trying to ignore the way he had her pulse racing. "Would that be so bad?"

"I never let anyone have the advantage."

"Maybe you should—think of all you're missing out on." She wasn't one for flings, but Niko was different. The push and pull of her common sense versus her desires raged war within her. Should she? Or shouldn't she? In the end, she threw caution to the wind and decided that for Niko, she just might make an exception.

"Sofia? Did you hear me?"

He'd been talking? Between the loud voices and the strums of the eight-piece band, not to mention her own riotous thoughts, she'd missed what he'd said. And that was a shame because she loved his voice that was heavily laden with a Greek accent.

"I'm sorry. I'm having trouble hearing you."

"Perhaps you'd care to stop by my suite. We could continue our conversation. It's much quieter there. Unless of course you'd care to dance the night away."

He was inviting her to his suite? Her immediate response was no. But, then again, after tonight he'd be gone. And tomorrow she'd be like Cinderella, trading in her royal blue chiffon gown and satin heels for a black-and-white maid's uniform complete with no-nonsense black shoes with rubber soles.

The way Niko implored her with his eyes eroded any lingering doubts. Tonight would be her fairy tale—something she'd remember for years to come.

"Lead the way."

CHAPTER ONE

Twelve weeks later...

HE WAS LATE.

He was never late. Nikolas Stravos III expelled a disgruntled sigh as he stood in the shower. There was something about being at the Blue Tide Resort that always seemed to have him acting out of character. His previous stay had included the most fascinating evening with the most incredible woman. He smiled at the memory.

He turned away from the spray of water, letting the soapsuds slide down his body. He leaned forward, pressing his palms against the cold tiles. The jets of water beat against the backs of his shoulders. Hundreds of droplets of water came together and trickled down his spine. He longed for the pulsating rhythm to ease away the ache in his tense muscles.

A lot had happened since he'd last been to the Blue Tide. He now had a solo voice in the operation and direction of the Stravos Trust, a position he'd been groomed to ascend to since childhood. But no one had warned him the promotion would cost him dearly.

It'd all started here at the resort, at Cristo Kiriakas's wedding to Kyra, Niko's newfound cousin. The memories unfolded in his mind like a promo to a blockbuster movie, hitting all the highlights.

Some of the recollections were amazing, like getting to know Sofia, the maid of honor. And spending a glorious night together, an evening he hadn't been able to banish from his mind. But as good as that brief period had been, what had followed was horrific—losing his grandfather suddenly to a heart attack. The memory still sliced through him. There had been no time for good-byes—no final words. It was all over before Niko had time to react.

He cursed under his breath as he turned off the water. Life could be so cruel sometimes. If he'd learned one thing, it was that everything could change at the drop of a hat. No notice. No nothing. And then you were all alone in this big, cold world. It was the story of his life.

Niko reached for the towel waiting for him just

outside the shower stall. Instead of thinking about his upcoming business meeting with Cristo to finalize the terms of the sale of the Stravos Star Hotels, Niko found his thoughts spiraling back to Sofia. He ran the plush towel over his face. He made a mental note to inquire about her. He hadn't even gotten a chance to learn where she lived. By the time he'd awoken on that not-so-long-ago morning, she was gone. Like a dream, she'd vanished—

Thunk!

The startling noise drew his thoughts up short. *What was that?* It sure sounded like something had fallen over. But how was that possible? He didn't recall leaving a window open for the breeze to wreak havoc. But he conceded that, in his exhausted state after working day and night, anything was possible. And he had opened the windows last night when he'd first arrived. Perhaps he'd forgotten to close one of them.

Not bothering to dry himself off, he draped the towel around his waist, anxious to find out what damage had been done. His feet moved soundlessly over the cool ceramic tile floor.

He stepped into the outer room when he heard, "Ghuahh!"

He stopped in his tracks. He scanned the room, at last settling on a most beautiful woman. Her eyes were round with alarm as she straightened, holding a lamp that belonged on the end table. Who was this woman? And what was she doing in his bungalow uninvited?

His gaze moved back to her face. It took a second before he realized he knew her—in fact, he knew her quite well, in a manner of speaking. Sofia. She'd come back. And this time, she wasn't a figment of his dreams. She was standing before him with those tempting lips and all her curvy goodness.

He noticed how her gaze slipped down to his towel before quickly returning to his face. Her cheeks were suffused with color. *Really?* How could she be so innocent after the night they'd spent together?

Still, at the sight of her embarrassment, he felt as though the towel had shrunk to half its size. He should have excused himself to go throw on some clothes, but his mind wasn't exactly working right. "Sofia? What are you doing here?"

Her mouth opened, but nothing came out. She turned and bolted for the door.

"Hey, wait!" He hadn't meant to scare her off.

Perhaps his tone hadn't exactly been welcoming, but she was in his bungalow without an invitation—oh, who was he kidding? He was frustrated with himself for being so excited to see her.

And he just couldn't let her get away without finding out why she'd sought him out. He started after her, but when he reached the covered porch of his exclusive bungalow, a breeze rushed past him, reminding him that he was dressed in nothing more than a bath towel.

He stopped and stared at Sofia's back as she moved away from him as quickly as her legs would carry her. What puzzled him the most was why she kept leaving him without so much as a word.

Usually he had the opposite problem with women. They were too clingy for his comfort. Sofia was different. She intrigued him. He'd have to work harder at making a good impression the next time they met.

He pressed his hand to the wooden rail as he watched her make her way along the path surrounded by lush, colorful vegetation. All too soon, she disappeared from sight. The part that stuck with him was the fact she'd been wearing a maid's uniform. *She works here?*

A whistle drew his attention. He turned to find a pretty brunette in a red bikini sunbathing not far from his bungalow. She flashed him a toothy smile and waved, but he didn't return the gesture, not wanting to encourage her attention.

His phone chimed with a reminder that he had a meeting in fifteen minutes. With a shake of his head, he turned and headed inside the thatched-roof bungalow. Thoughts of Sofia persisted. Had she, too, been unable to forget about their time together? Was that why she'd shown up at his bungalow? But if so, why had she run away? Surely it wasn't his lack of clothing. It had to be more than that. But what?

He inwardly groaned as he removed the first suit he came across in the wardrobe. His knowledge of women wouldn't even fill up a shot glass. And he had no intention of learning more—at least not anytime soon. And when he did decide to settle down, it would be a marriage of convenience.

He'd experienced enough loss in his life. He wasn't about to risk his heart on romance. A strategically planned marriage would be best for all concerned. It's what made the most sense. From what he'd observed, emotions were too fickle. Sometimes he wondered if romantic love truly existed or if people only imagined it. He sighed. Even if it did exist, he was better off without such an entanglement. It just made life more complicated than it needed to be.

If he were smart, he'd forget Sofia. That was the best thing he could do for both of them, because he had nothing to offer her except a moment here or a moment there. Certainly nothing consistent— nothing lasting.

In fact, tomorrow he would be jetting off, far from the Blue Tide Resort. His grandfather had given him one last mission to complete. And that had to be Niko's focus—not a beautiful woman with eyes full of mystery.

Her heart pounded.

Sofia pressed a hand to her chest as she eased open the door to the employee area in the lower level of the resort. With it being midmorning, the locker area was deserted. Everyone was busy trying to get their assigned tasks completed while the guests soaked up rays on the beach, golfed or toured the picturesque seaside.

She moved to the far corner of the room, anxious to be alone. Her mind had been racing ever since she ran into Mr. Dreamy, as she'd dubbed him during her best friend's wedding. What was he doing back here? And why hadn't Kyra mentioned his visit?

Sofia leaned against the cool tiled wall. She slid down to the floor and pulled out her phone. She could really use a sounding board. It wasn't until then that she realized her hands were trembling.

She didn't know what she'd been expecting for their reunion, but it certainly wasn't the suspicion in Niko's eyes. And when he spoke, his voice had been laced with agitation.

The backs of her eyes stung, and her stomach churned. This couldn't be happening. She hadn't meant to catch him by surprise. There had been no privacy notice on the door, and she'd knocked several times without getting a response. She hadn't even known that he'd returned to the Blue Tide.

Her fingers moved over the keyboard as she messaged Kyra.

MaidintheShade347 (Sofia): He's here!

Seconds passed and nothing. She willed Kyra to message her back. Of all the times she needed her best friend... Sofia's hand moved protectively over her still-flat midsection.

"It's okay, little one. I'll get this all sorted out.

I promise." Impatiently her fingers moved over the keypad again.

MaidintheShade347 (Sofia): I need you.

Mop&Glow007 (Kyra): I'm here. Who's here?

MaidintheShade347 (Sofia): Niko. What do I do?

Mop&Glow007 (Kyra): Do you want to see him?

Sofia hadn't told Kyra the steamy bits that had transpired between her and Niko. It felt strange to hold back from her best friend, who until this point in her life had known all her secrets and insecurities. But this was different. She'd had a one-night stand with Niko—Kyra's long-lost cousin. That totally changed the rules of the game.

There was something else Sofia hadn't told Kyra—she was pregnant. Sofia had just found out earlier that week. She would tell Kyra everything just as soon as she figured out how best to deal with Niko.

MaidintheShade347 (Sofia): No. Yes. I don't know.

Mop&Glow007 (Kyra): Do you want me to say something to him for you?

MaidintheShade347 (Sofia): No!

Mop&Glow007 (Kyra): Are you sure?

MaidintheShade347 (Sofia): I'll handle it.

Mop&Glow007 (Kyra): LMK if you change your mind. I'll help.

The offer was generous, so typical of Kyra. Her friend had already pulled strings and gotten Sofia enrolled in an in-house managerial training program. Sofia was immensely grateful for the opportunity, but she was seriously considering returning to the States to earn an accounting degree. She'd always had a knack for numbers.

Though Kyra's offer to help smooth over things with Niko was tempting, Sofia would have to face Niko on her own. She couldn't even imagine how he'd react to her news.

CHAPTER TWO

NIKO YANKED AT his necktie, loosening it. He took the steps leading up to his bungalow two at a time while holding firmly to the notes he'd taken during his meeting with Cristo. He released the top buttons on his dress shirt. Whatever made him think wearing a suit at the Blue Tide was a good idea?

Because it was a habit. He felt in control in a suit and tie. His grandfather had drilled this message into him since he was just a boy. Without his father around to assume his rightful place as the Stravos heir, the role had fallen to Niko. He'd vowed at an early age to be the type of man that would have made his father and grandfather proud. That role included dressing the part.

However, Cristo hadn't felt the need for business attire, even though they were dealing with a very big contract that involved the sale of Niko's international hotel chain to Cristo. Thankfully the meeting had gone quite well. The changes to the terms of the contract were minor. So why was he so uptight? So out of sorts?

The answer immediately came to him in the vision of Sofia. He strode into the bungalow, where he uncharacteristically tossed his tie over the back of the couch, followed by his suit jacket. Why had she looked at him as if he were the Big Bad Wolf and she were Little Red Riding Hood? Had he really been that gruff?

He gave himself a mental shake as he sat down at the spacious desk and turned on his laptop. He'd be lost without it. Immediately his email software popped up on the screen. Forty-three new emails since that morning. All appeared to be business related. He inwardly groaned. They'd have to wait a little longer.

Niko opened a new email and started typing a note to his legal team. Sofia's panic-stricken face as she'd rushed out the door came to him. He shoved the image to the back of his mind as he transcribed his hasty notes into something more understandable.

When he'd finished proofreading the rather lengthy email, he pressed Send. He soon found three more emails had landed in his inbox. He leaned back in his chair as the memory of Sofia continued to plague him.

What had she wanted? Why had she looked so upset? He couldn't fully focus on his work until he had answers.

Niko strode over to the phone and was quickly connected with the front desk. He couldn't come straight out and request they send over Sofia. It would raise too many questions. Instead he requested the maid who'd cleaned his room to stop by, as he'd misplaced some papers and needed to know if she'd seen them. He assured the desk clerk that no crime had been committed. He just needed a bit of help.

Not more than five minutes later, there was a knock at the door. Niko opened it to find Sofia holding a stack of plush white towels as though they were a shield. "Hi. Thanks for coming back."

Her gaze didn't quite meet his. "I...I didn't see any papers."

He arched a brow. "And you would know this how? You took off so fast this morning that you didn't have time to look around."

"I'm sorry about that. I didn't know you were in the bungalow."

After being up late into the night working, he'd

slept in. He'd forgotten to put out the do-not-disturb placard. That answered some of his questions but not all of them. "I understand about the mix-up this morning, but we still need to talk."

Panic reflected in her brown eyes. "We...we do."

He got the feeling from her awkward stance and the way her gaze didn't quite meet his that whatever she had to say he wasn't going to like it. Not one little bit. It was like he'd walked in on the middle of a play and he had absolutely no idea what was going on.

If he was smart, he'd just make a quick excuse to disentangle himself from Sofia right here and now. But what came out of his mouth was something entirely different. "Come inside."

She hesitated before moving past him, taking great pains to keep some distance between them. This was not the way he'd expected her to act after their amazing night together. In fact, it was exactly the opposite.

When she stood in the middle of the living room, clenching and unclenching her hands, he said, "You can have a seat."

She perched on the edge of the couch. She laced

her fingers together and rested them in her lap. The awkward silence stretched out.

"What did you want to discuss?" Surely it couldn't be as serious as her body language indicated. Perhaps she regretted running out on him the morning after the wedding and she wanted to know if they could start over.

The thought of letting her down weighed on him. He'd really enjoyed getting to know her. She'd been so easy to be around. But as amazing as he found her, he wasn't at a place in his life where he could even think about a serious relationship. Maybe it wasn't right—wasn't fair—but neither would lying to her. In the end, it would hurt her more.

His gaze met hers. There was a vulnerability in her eyes that evoked a protective side of him he hadn't been aware of before that moment. Her eyes grew shiny as though she were about to burst into tears at any moment.

No. Please. Not that.

Niko sat down on an adjacent armchair, uncomfortable with the thought of dealing with an emotional woman. He had absolutely no experience in that area. He wasn't a love-'em-and-leave-'em kinda guy. But on the rare occasions he spent the evening in a woman's company, whether for a fund-raiser or a business dinner, he made sure she knew up front that there would never be anything serious between them.

Had he told Sofia that? His memory was a bit fuzzy. He remembered when he'd first approached her at the wedding reception. She'd been sitting all alone at the bridal table. He'd been drawn to her, unable to resist talking to her.

Her smile had been the first thing he noticed. It had lit up her whole face, and it was infectious. The evening had been full of dancing and sparkling wine. Then more dancing, more laughing and more wine. He honestly hadn't wanted the night to end.

The woman sitting before him didn't resemble the engaging, bubbly woman at his cousin's wedding—she may look the same, but it was obvious something major had changed. What could it be? Why did she look as though she had the weight of the world on her delicate shoulders?

He drew his thoughts up short. Whatever was bothering her, he wasn't the one to resolve it. As much as he wanted to ride to her rescue, he was only in town for the night. There simply wasn't enough time—or so he tried to tell himself.

* * *

Sofia had no idea why Niko had requested her presence. Obviously, it wasn't to locate any missing papers or to restock his towels. Realizing she was still holding the fresh linens, she placed them on the couch next to her. She knew for a fact he had more than enough fresh towels because once he'd departed the bungalow that morning, she'd rushed back in. She'd done her fastest, most thorough cleaning job to date. So whatever he wanted had absolutely nothing to do with housekeeping.

And by the serious look on his face, he wasn't anxious to pick up where they'd left off. So where did that leave them? Was he just upset about finding her in his room? Or did he know about her pregnancy? No, impossible. She hadn't told a soul.

The best course of action was to get it all out there in the open, but her mouth refused to cooperate. She could feel Niko's gaze on her, and she averted her eyes to the pattern on the rug. Her stomach quivered.

Why was she letting herself get all twisted up in knots? It wasn't as if she wanted anything from him. Quite the contrary. She planned to take care of the baby on her own.

Niko cleared his throat. "Listen, I know you

probably came here expecting us to pick up where we left off—"

"What? No, I didn't." Was that what he was expecting? Another clandestine hookup before he left?

His eyes widened. "You didn't?"

"What do you take me for?" Sofia pressed her lips together, holding back a stinging comment. Just because he was sexy and rich didn't mean she was going to throw herself at him. Was that how little he thought of her?

"I apologize if I jumped to the wrong conclusion." The look in his eyes said he didn't quite believe her. "Then why did you agree that we needed to talk?"

"I...I..." Her stomach lurched nauseously.

She jumped to her feet, not about to get sick in front of him. It was time to make a hasty exit. She would admit to her pregnancy later, when she wasn't so nervous. She rushed to the door. She could hear Niko curse under his breath as he hurried after her.

"Sofia, wait!"

She stopped at the edge of the porch. She inhaled a couple of deep breaths. Her stomach settled a bit. Her hands gripped the wood and squeezed tight, willing herself to remain calm enough to utter words.

"I need to tell you something." So far so good. Now if only she could get the rest out. "It's about the night of the wedding."

"It's okay." He stopped just behind her. His voice was much softer than it had been just moments before. "I understand. I haven't been able to forget that night, either."

"You haven't?" She turned, finding him much closer than she'd expected. That was not what she was expecting him to say.

His voice lowered and vibrated with emotion. "No, I haven't. It was special." He stared deep into her eyes. "You are special. But after you disappeared without a word, I thought you regretted it."

Her heart leaped into her throat. Was this really happening? Was it possible she'd totally misjudged him? "You really mean it? About the special part?"

His head dipped, and his lips claimed hers. There was no room for doubt in his kiss. This was how she remembered things from that one magical night. Maybe it'd been the sparkling wine or the romantic ballads, but Niko had swept her off her feet…just like now.

His lips moved over hers, brushing aside the rush of turbulent emotions and replacing them with pure, undiluted passion. She suddenly remembered how on that not-so-long-ago night she'd momentarily disengaged from her common sense and followed her heart. Their time together wasn't supposed to be anything serious, but sometimes actions have consequences. And in her—well, their—case, it was a life-altering consequence.

But as his hands moved over her back, her stiff muscles eased. Her body leaned into his. Her hands wrapped around the back of his neck as her fingertips played with the longer strands of his dark hair. She could easily get used to this— quite easy indeed.

Thunk!

Sofia jumped back as though the bungalow had been struck by lightning. She glanced around. Her gaze came to rest on a volleyball. A couple of teenage girls came rushing up to the bungalow and apologized. Niko smiled, flashing his white teeth, and assured them it wasn't a problem. Just as if nothing had happened.

Sofia tried to wrap her mind around how things had gotten so far off course. Her hand moved to her lips, her fingers gently swiping over her now-sensitive lips. Though her heart fluttered at the memory of their kiss, she knew she had to show more self-restraint. Giving in to her desires had succeeded only in complicating matters even more.

Her attention moved to the steps. She wanted to flee—wanted to avoid the inevitable questions—

"Don't even think about escaping. I'm dressed this time. I'll follow you."

CHAPTER THREE

"THAT KISS...IT CAN'T happen again." Sofia met his confused gaze.

Best to get this over with.

The sooner, the better.

Her palms moistened, and her mouth grew dry. She had no idea how much longer she could stand to be so close to him and yet so far away. Because she knew her secret would drive a permanent wedge between them. Nothing would ever be the same.

His expression hardened. "Then what exactly did you want to talk about?"

The time had come. Her stomach took another nervous lurch. And the words that she'd rehearsed over and over again utterly fled her mind.

"Sofia?"

It wasn't as if she'd gotten into this position by herself. And though it was the truth, it didn't settle her nerves. Why did this have to be so hard? Because he'd blame her. His eyes would grow dark and cold, shutting her out.

Niko made a point of glancing at his Rolex watch. "I don't have much time. Maybe we should talk later—"

"No!" When he frowned, she realized her response had been a bit too exuberant.

He arched a dark brow. "It's that important?"

She nodded, not trusting her mouth.

"Then come back inside."

She did as he asked. It was just two words— *I'm pregnant.* Why did she have to make such a production of this?

Just say the words and leave. Easy. Peasy. Not!

He moved to the minibar. "Can I get you something to drink? A mimosa?"

She shook her head. She couldn't drink in her condition. Instead of taking advantage of the opening, she said, "I can't. I'm still working. Some water would be nice."

In no time at all, he was handing her a glass of ice water. "Now, what did you need to talk about?"

She sipped at the water, needing it to wet her dry mouth. Once she set it aside, she clenched her hands and faced him. "I'm pregnant."

For a moment, nothing moved. It was as if time were suspended. As the seconds ticked by, the color leached from Niko's face.

At last he spoke in a strangled voice. "It...it's mine?"

"Of course it's yours. You surely don't think I have sex with every man I meet."

He raked his fingers through his hair. "How should I know?"

She glared at him. "That doesn't say much for you."

"You're right. I'm sorry. I'm not thinking clearly." He started to pace back and forth. "I just never thought." He stopped and stared at her as though expecting an answer. "But how could this happen?"

She frowned at him. Was their night so forgettable? Her face warmed at the memory. Did she really have to recount the evening in detail for him?

He shook his head. "Never mind. It was a stupid question. I...I'm just shocked. We took precaution."

"And it failed somewhere along the way. But analyzing the how of it isn't going to change the fact. What is done is done."

His face grew even paler. "Things did get pretty out of hand that night."

That was the understatement of the century. She'd never thought she'd ever have a one-night stand in her life, but that was before she met Niko. He was a mixture of hotness, sweetness and power wrapped up in a really cute package.

Funnily enough, telling him the news of the baby had a calming effect on her. She had not been expecting that. Perhaps it was because she was no longer harboring a huge, life-changing secret. With the truth out in the open, they could make whatever decisions were necessary.

"You're sure about this?" He gazed at her with one last bit of hope glimmering in his eyes.

She nodded. "I went to the doctor this week. He confirmed what I suspected."

Niko's shoulders slumped. "Oh."

She felt bad for him. He obviously wasn't looking to start a family anytime soon, and she had blindsided him with this news. She hadn't known any other way to tell him. She knew it wouldn't be unreasonable to expect him to step up and take responsibility. But that wasn't why she'd told him. As the father he had a right to know.

"Listen, I know this isn't what you want."

His head snapped around to face her. His dark brows rose high as his gaze searched hers. "And it's what you want?"

She wasn't about to get into what she did and didn't want. Ideally she wanted to be in love with the father of her baby, and even though they'd shared an incredibly intense attraction, she refused to let herself believe in love at first sight. Whatever she'd felt for Niko at the wedding had been an intense attraction. Nothing more.

She stared deep into his eyes and swallowed hard. "I'm keeping the baby if that's what you mean."

His expression didn't give away his thoughts. "I'll need some time to digest this."

"That's fair." There was one more thing she hadn't told him. "How much time are we talking?"

He raked his fingers through his hair. "I don't know. Why?"

"I'm leaving in two weeks."

"Leaving?"

She nodded. "I'd appreciate it if you didn't tell anyone, as I haven't turned in my notice yet."

"Leaving and going where?"

"Home. Back to New York. I want my baby—"

"Our baby."

She sighed. "Our baby to grow up around family."

His mouth opened, but before he could utter a word, her phone chimed. It was the ringtone she'd assigned to her boss. Although this was a bad time for a phone call, she couldn't ignore it, either.

Her gaze met Niko's. "It's my supervisor."

Niko's lips pressed together as he waved at her to go ahead and answer it. Was it her imagination or was he relieved by the distraction? There was no time for her to contemplate it as the phone chimed again.

She pressed the button, knowing her absence had been noticed and she didn't have a good excuse. Or at least not one that she was willing to share.

She moved to the porch for some privacy. "Hello."

This can't be happening.

Alone now, Niko paced back and forth. Sofia had appeared more than relieved to be summoned back to work. He glanced down at the scrap of paper where she'd jotted down her phone number and told him to call her when he was ready to talk.

Talk? He couldn't think straight much less string together a bunch of coherent sentences. Not so long ago, he'd had his life planned out. But in a matter of weeks, twelve to be exact, it'd all gone off course.

First, his grandfather unexpectedly passed away and now he was about to become a father. *A father.* The words sounded so off to him. He wasn't ready to be a father. What did he even know about being a parent? *Nothing. Zip. Zilch. And nada.*

And to think that not so long ago this news would have been the answer to so many of his problems with his grandfather. The thought of not being able to share this news with him sent a fresh wave of sorrow washing over Niko. His hands balled up at his sides as he struggled to control his rising emotions.

His cell phone rang, but he ignored it—something he rarely did. He wasn't in any frame of mind to talk business. He wasn't sure how it felt to be in shock, but he'd hazard a guess it was what he was experiencing now.

The truth was he wasn't ready to be a family man.

He had too much to do…like restructuring the numerous divisions to eliminate overlap of personnel and continuing to overhaul his outdated company with new human resources policies. Even though he'd faced employee pushback in the face of change, he refused to let that stop him. He wasn't the boss in order to win friends. He'd been groomed to lead the company into the future. To do that, change must be a part of his plan.

But how was he supposed to fit a baby into that plan?

He accepted that someday he'd need an heir or two to hand down the family business. That was in his plan—his long-range plan. But a family didn't fit in his agenda now.

Still, there was a baby on the way. That couldn't be changed. Nor could he turn his back on his own flesh and blood. For the first time in his life, he didn't know which way to turn. The stakes were just too high.

His grandfather's solution would have been to have a wedding—quick and simple. He imagined how his grandfather would pat him on the back, pleased that he was carrying on the Stravos line. But would his parents have been just as pleased? Or would they have been disappointed in him? The thought weighed heavily on him. He missed them, especially at a time like this.

So what options did that leave him? To marry Sofia? But was it the right decision? Could Sofia be his convenient bride? Would she accept an unconventional marriage?

He recalled her contagious laughter at the wedding—the way she'd turned his head. She'd been like a breath of fresh air, and he'd been unable to get enough of her.

Could they ever get back to that happy place? He'd like to think once the shock wore away that they could smile and laugh again—together. So maybe the idea of marriage had come much sooner than he expected. He and Sofia had hit it off. He may not want a romantic entanglement, but he would like them to be on friendly terms when they wed. And the fact they were compatible in bed was a definite bonus.

Would Sofia jump at the offer? Or would she rebuff his proposal? The one thing he'd learned about Sofia was that she could be unpredictable, which made her quite intriguing. But it also left him uncertain when it came to his proposition of a marriage in name only.

Certain that he was on to something, he called Cristo. Luckily, his friend had just wrapped up a meeting. He was available to have coffee and a chat. Though Cristo asked him repeatedly if there was a problem, Niko was reluctant to get into it over the phone. This delicate conversation needed to be handled in person. And even then Niko was hesitant to share the full details—only what was necessary to bring his quickly evolving plan to fruition.

CHAPTER FOUR

THIS PLAN JUST had to work.

Niko stepped inside Cristo's luxury suite. Not so long ago they'd met here to discuss business, but this time his agenda was a bit more personal. Over the months, he and Cristo had become not only family, but also close friends. It was interesting to both of them how much they had in common—powerful families with unrealistic expectations.

Niko joined Cristo on his private balcony overlooking the beach littered with sunbathers soaking up the sunshine while others enjoyed the warm water of the resort's private cove. They all looked so relaxed and happy. Right now, Niko couldn't remember what it was like to be either of those two things.

His gut knotted up. If he made the wrong decision, he knew it would impact not only his life but Sofia's and their unborn baby's. The decision to make Sofia his bride didn't have to be made overnight. If he cut his trip short, Sofia would still be at the Blue Tide when he returned.

Cristo cleared his throat. "Sorry about the delay. Some staffing issues were just brought to my attention."

"You really take a hands-on approach with this place, don't you?"

Cristo poured them each a cup of coffee. "Yes. This resort is special to me. It was my idea. I've seen it through the planning, building and opening. And now that Kyra and I married here, it's our home."

"Even more so than New York?"

"My home is wherever my wife is, and right now, she's enjoying her time here." Cristo sipped his coffee. "So tell me what's on your mind."

Niko wasn't sure how much of what he was thinking he should vocalize. "I wanted to ask you about Sofia."

A knowing smile came across Cristo's face. "I saw the way you two hit it off at the wedding. Kyra wanted to do some matchmaking, but I told her not to get involved. It's better when things work out on their own. So you and Sofia, are you getting serious?"

Now how exactly did he answer that? The pregnancy was serious. The rest of it had yet to be determined. "We might be."

"And that's why you're here? You want to know if there's any reason you shouldn't get involved?"

Niko inclined his head. "Something like that."

Cristo took another sip of his coffee. "I don't know if I'm the person you should consult."

"Why's that?"

"Because I know nothing about romance and relationships."

"But how can that be? You're happily married."

"And that's due to my amazing wife. She's the one who believed in us and helped me to get past some rough spots. If it wasn't for her, I'd still be miserable and alone."

That last comment really caught Niko's attention. "You were miserable when you were single?"

Cristo shrugged his shoulders. "I just didn't want to admit it to myself. I thought I knew what would make me happy. And I was completely wrong. Lucky for me, Kyra opened my eyes. Your cousin is very smart, but if you tell her I said any of this, I'll totally deny it."

A smile pulled at Niko's lips. "Don't worry. I don't think I have to tell my cousin a thing. Anyone can see the happiness radiating from you two."

"It's easy when you have the right person in your life. Do you think Sofia is the right person for you?"

The smile slipped from Niko's face. "I think so."

"Why do you look so worried?"

"I'm not sure Sofia feels the same way."

"Ah, I understand. Women are tough to read."

Niko cleared his throat. "Speaking of Sofia, have you known her long?"

"Depends on how you look at it. I've known her as long as I've known Kyra. And that was long enough for me to realize I wasn't going to let Kyra get away. From what I've witnessed, Sofia is loyal and trustworthy."

"Thanks for the insight."

"But if you're curious about Sofia, why aren't you talking to her?"

Cristo was right. He just wanted to make sure there wasn't something he was missing about Sofia before he enacted his plan. "It's just that... Oh, never mind. I need to focus on my trip so we can finalize our deal. I'll worry about this stuff later."

"How long will you be gone?"

"Not long." While away, he intended to give his

idea of marriage to Sofia some serious thought. "A few weeks."

"That fast?"

"You sound surprised." To him, being away from the Stravos Trust during this pivotal transition seemed like an eternity.

"I don't know. I just thought you might want to take some downtime after everything that has happened."

He was referring to the death of Niko's grandfather. "I did take a little time off, but I found the work helps. It's therapeutic for me."

Cristo nodded in understanding. "Maybe the trip will be good for you, too."

"Honestly, I'm not thrilled about this trip. It couldn't have come at a worse time."

"Then why not delay it?"

"Trust me—the thought has crossed my mind more than once. But the sale of the hotel chain can't be delayed. I have plans for the money, and I'm sure you're anxious to get on with the merger of the two hotel chains."

"When are you leaving?"

"Tomorrow."

"And what about Sofia? You don't want to miss this opportunity. You might never get it back."

Cristo's warning made Niko hesitate. Had he somehow found out about Sofia's plans to return to New York? She'd said she hadn't turned her resignation in yet, but after their discussion perhaps she'd changed her mind. "Is there a particular reason you say that?"

Cristo rubbed his clean-shaven jaw. "I really shouldn't say anything—"

"This is important. If it's about Sofia, I really need to know."

Cristo's brows rose. "Fine. The phone call I was on when you arrived was from my manager. Sofia has tendered her resignation at the Blue Tide Resort. She's transferring back to the New York hotel."

"How soon?"

"Immediately."

"Immediately?" This was news.

"I haven't spoken to her myself, but from what I can gather, she's planning to hop on the next plane to New York. You wouldn't know anything about that, would you?"

"Let's just say I might have some idea about what's going on." When Cristo sent him an *I knew it* look, Niko continued, "The thing is I, um, need her help. Would it be possible to give her some time off?"

"What sort of time are we talking? A day? Or two?"

"At least a few weeks."

Cristo's eyes widened. "I see. Well, I think we could make that work. But is Sofia willing to go along with whatever you have in mind?"

"I don't know, but I'm about to find out."

"Are you sure—"

"I am." Niko jumped to his feet. "Thanks. I have to go."

He didn't have a specific plan in mind to delay her departure, but he'd think of something. He didn't have a choice. He couldn't let Sofia disappear before they settled things. He was good at coming up with spontaneous plans. He had to come up with something good, something irresistible.

With a sigh, Sofia settled on the couch in her efficiency apartment. It had been a long, stressful day, and all she wanted now was to stay put, eat some leftover pizza and watch a romantic comedy. It might cheer her up. Then again, an adventure movie might be better.

Her meeting with Niko hadn't gone terribly wrong, but it hadn't been good, either. Was it so far-fetched that she'd secretly envisioned his happy acceptance of the news? Instead, Niko looked as though he'd been diagnosed with a month to live.

Sofia glanced down at the uneaten slice of pepperoni pizza in her hand. Her stomach lurched. She slipped the food back on the plate. Maybe she'd finish it later—much later. After her stomach stopped feeling as if it was on the high seas. She hadn't experienced morning sickness until this week. Perhaps it was her nerves. Whatever it was, she wanted it to go away.

When her phone chimed, she welcomed the distraction. She snatched it from the coffee table, expecting to find a text from Kyra. Sofia had messaged her best friend earlier, telling her they needed to talk ASAP.

She'd been best friends with Kyra since junior high. Sofia thought they complemented each other well. She liked to take risks while Kyra liked to toe the line. Between the two of them, they'd kept out of trouble—or at least were never caught, as Kyra had reminded her over the years. But still, having a baby with a man that Kyra was just getting to know as family might put a strain on their friendship. Sofia hoped she was worried for nothing, but she'd learned the hard way that things don't always work out the way you imagine.

When she glanced at her phone, she saw the message wasn't from Kyra, after all. It was Niko. Her heart pounded, and her palms grew clammy. She immediately clicked on the text, anxious to find out what he wanted.

NikoStravosIII: Can we meet?

MaidintheShade347 (Sofia): When?

NikoStravosIII: Now.

She glanced down at her gray sweat shorts and faded pink T-shirt. She definitely wasn't in any condition to run out the door and meet up with a billionaire. She wondered if he ever had a hair out of place or dressed in anything but designer clothes. She highly doubted it.

MaidintheShade347 (Sofia): Now isn't a good time.

NikoStravosIII: It has to be tonight.

MaidintheShade347 (Sofia): I don't know.

NikoStravosIII: We must talk before you leave tomorrow.

He knew? At least it saved her from having to tell him. And as much as she hated to admit it, he was right. They had to finish their discussion, and perhaps it'd be easier in person. But he wouldn't change her mind—she was going home. She'd just heard about an opening at the hotel in New York, and she'd jumped on it. It would make it possible for her to make a future for her and the baby near her family.

MaidintheShade347 (Sofia): Can you give me a little time?

NikoStravosIII: Hurry.

MaidintheShade347 (Sofia): I will.

Sofia leaped up from the couch. After tossing her leftover pizza back in the fridge, she hurried to her small bedroom. A glance in the mirror told her that she would benefit from jumping in the shower and starting all over again, but she knew Niko wouldn't have the patience to wait that long. So she'd have to do her best to quickly paste herself back together.

At last she settled for a short summer dress that had a sleeveless denim blouse that tied at the waist and a white flowered skirt. It looked good on her without letting on that she'd tried too hard. After all, this wasn't a date or anything.

She texted Niko when she was ready. He wanted to meet on the beach. It was evening now, and the resort's guests would be having dinner. For the most part, they'd have the beach to themselves.

She rushed out the door, all the while wondering what he'd decided. As she rode down the elevator by herself, she pressed a protective hand to her abdomen and whispered, "Don't worry, little one. Everything will be all right." If only she could convince herself of that. "Your daddy will see that I'm doing what's best for all concerned."

Sofia made her way from the small employee complex on the outskirts of the resort to the hotel. It wasn't until then that she realized Niko hadn't been explicit in his instructions. The beach was huge. But she didn't have to wonder for long as he waved to her.

She joined him on the overlook that gave a stunning view of the private cove. The setting sun splashed streaks of pink and purple over the darkening water. But it wasn't the horizon that made the breath catch in Sofia's throat.

Her gaze settled on Niko. His wavy hair was finger-combed back off his face. Talk about hitting the jackpot in the gene department. If their baby took after him, it'd be adorable.

Niko was wearing dark slacks and a blue dress shirt. Didn't the man ever go casual? She was starting to wonder if his wardrobe contained anything but designer suits. Although tonight he'd dispensed with his jacket and tie. The sleeves of his shirt were rolled up, and the top buttons were undone, giving a hint of the few dark curls on his chest. Her fingers longed to reach out to him as she had on that unforgettable night.

Her gaze rose, meeting his. A frown pulled at his lips as he glanced down at himself. "Is there something wrong with my clothes?"

Realizing that she'd been caught staring, she shook her head. "Um…no."

"Are you sure? Did I spill something on myself?"

She shook her head again. "I was just wondering if you ever wear anything but suits."

"Really? That's what you were thinking?" When

she nodded, he added, "And what's wrong with a suit?"

She waved her hand around at the beach. "You do realize this is a resort. People come here to relax and unwind. You look like you're ready to close a billion-dollar deal."

"Ah, but in my case I came to the Blue Tide Resort to do exactly that." He smiled, sending her stomach dipping. "Well, not the billion-dollar part, but it's a substantial deal. Therefore, my attire is quite appropriate."

"Are you always so uptight? Do you ever kick back? Relax?"

"Of course."

She didn't believe him. "I think you focus on business 24/7."

"Did you ever consider I might find it relaxing?"

"And the suits?"

"To quote my grandfather, a man must dress properly to do business. But if you hadn't noticed, I did dispense with my jacket and tie."

She shook her head in disbelief. Inside, her stomach shivered with nervous tension. Critiquing his attire wasn't why he'd invited her here, but she welcomed the diversion. "How about some jean shorts and a T-shirt? Or in your case, perhaps dress shorts and a polo shirt?"

He glanced away. "I'm more comfortable like this."

"Do you even own any casual clothes?"

"Of course." He responded much too quickly, making her wonder whether he really did own anything she would classify as casual. "But I just returned from a meeting."

Was it really his clothes that bothered her? Or was it the thought that if she dressed him down, then his attitude might not be so serious? She wasn't quite sure. "Did you pack any of these casual clothes?"

"As a matter of fact, I did."

"Good. I'll wait here while you go change."

"Change? Why would I do that?"

"So we can go for a walk on the beach."

His hesitant gaze moved to the deserted beach and then back at her. "Wouldn't you be more comfortable talking here? We could order dinner and eat on the terrace."

He wanted to talk and eat? Her stomach lurched. There was no way. Walking and talking was much more appealing. "I'm not hungry." She didn't even want to smell food at this point. "I'd really like to walk."

He looked at her closely. "Are you feeling all right?"

She nodded.

"You're sure? You look a little pale."

She frowned. "Well, thank you. That's always what a woman wants to hear."

"I didn't mean it like that. I just meant… Oh, never mind. Wait here. I'll be right back."

She nodded, but still he hesitated. "I'll wait. I promise."

His eyes said that he didn't trust her. At all. "Good. We have important issues to discuss."

She couldn't tell by the tone of his voice if she was going to like what he had to say or not. At this point, she wasn't even sure what she wanted him to say. The push and pull of her conflicting emotions made her temples start to throb.

It will all work out. It will all work out.

She turned back to the view of the cove. All the while, she kept repeating those five words like some sort of mantra. It helped calm her nerves. Or so she wanted to believe.

She took in the colorful sky and the gentle lapping of the water. This was the kind of setting for a romantic movie where the hero and heroine walk off into the sunset. She inwardly groaned. That would never be her and Niko.

About to admit her mistake, she spun around to tell Niko that she'd changed her mind, but he was already gone. Whatever she did this evening, she had to keep her wits about her. Nothing good would come of repeating that toe-curling kiss. Nothing at all.

Still, her mind dwelled on that moment at his bungalow when he'd held her in his arms. Her heart picked up its pace. She'd never been kissed with such passion. No one had ever made her feel as if she was the only woman in the world for him—

No! No! No! she scolded herself. It didn't help when she recalled how delicious it was having his lips pressed to hers. She had to resist the temptation. She had to.

Somehow…

CHAPTER FIVE

SINCE WHEN DID he take orders?

He was the boss. He handed out the orders.

Niko glanced at Sofia. What was it about her that had him continually making exceptions to the rules?

The shorts and polo shirt he now wore were the only casual clothes he'd brought with him. To be honest, he wasn't quite sure what had possessed him to toss them into his suitcase. It must have been the fact that he liked to be prepared for any occasion. Although there was nothing in his suitcase to prepare him for a discussion about his baby—his baby—the words echoed in his mind.

"Niko?" Sofia's voice drew him from his thoughts.

Had she been speaking? He hadn't heard a word she'd said. That wasn't like him. He was good at multitasking, especially at business meetings. He could respond to emails on his phone while listening to a presentation and never lose a beat.

THE GREEK'S
NINE-MONTH
SURPRISE

But when he was around Sofia, he had problems staying on task.

"What did you say?"

"I asked if your business meeting went well."

He nodded. "It would have gone better if I'd been able to close the deal then and there."

"Why couldn't you?"

He didn't want to get into any of that now. They had other things to discuss. "That's not important." He stopped walking and turned to her. "We need to talk about your situation."

"You mean my pregnancy."

"Yes. That." She said it so easily, as if she'd already come to terms with it all. Was it possible she was happy about it? Could that be? "What are you planning to do? Because if you need—"

"I don't need anything. I already told you—I'm keeping it."

He frowned. "I don't know what you thought I was about to say. And I don't want to know. However, if you had let me finish, I was going to ask if I could help with your medical expenses."

He wanted only the best for her and their baby. Her vehement devotion to keeping their baby struck him. How had she become so attached and protective in such a short amount of time?

It must be different for mothers, because he was still struggling to wrap his mind around the whole baby issue. A baby. His baby. It still didn't feel real.

Curious about her acceptance of the situation, he asked, "How long have you known that you are pregnant?"

"I told you—I found out this week." She turned and started walking again, farther from the resort.

That's right. He vaguely remembered her mentioning it earlier that day, but he'd been too shocked for it to stick. "If it's all new to you, how can you be so certain you want this baby? It's going to change your entire world. Nothing will be the same."

"The timing might not be the best, but I always hoped that someday I'd be a mother." Her hand moved to her abdomen. Then, as though she realized what she was doing, she lowered her hand to her side. "But I understand that just because I feel this way doesn't mean you feel the same way. And…and I'm okay with that. We can say our goodbyes and—"

"Hold on. I didn't say anything about saying goodbye." She was the mother of his baby—the

Stravos heir. Like it or not, their lives were intricately entwined.

She turned to him, her eyes flashing with surprise. "So this means that you, um…want to be involved with the baby?"

That's what surprised her? "It is my baby—"

"Our baby."

He was going to have to work on that. He wasn't used to sharing anything with anyone. As an only child, he hadn't had the luxury of a sibling. As an adult, he'd never ventured into a committed relationship. So sharing was a new concept to him, but he would excel at it just like he did with everything he tackled in the boardroom. And by the stubborn look on Sofia's face, he didn't have any choice in the matter.

"How can you be so sure that being a mother at this stage in your life is the right thing to do?"

She glanced at him. "You really want to know?"

There was so much about her he wanted to know, but this was a good starting point. "Is it wrong for me to be curious?"

"No. But I'll warn you, it isn't what you're thinking. I don't want the baby because of who its father is. I want this baby for itself."

The conviction in her voice had him wanting

to believe her. But could he trust her? "You still didn't answer the question."

She sighed. "It all started when I met who I thought was the most wonderful guy. He was cute and charming. In fact, he ticked all of the boxes in what I thought I wanted in a man. He was a hard worker with a bright future in his uncle's construction firm."

"I take it he wasn't all you thought he'd be?"

She shook her head. "At the time, I worked as a housekeeper at the Glamour Hotel in New York. A lot of times our schedules didn't line up, so we'd go long stretches without seeing each other. As time went on, he seemed to work longer and longer hours."

Niko could relate with her ex. It was easy to get caught up in one's work. He did it all the time. But something told him there was more to Sofia's story than she'd revealed so far.

"My family immediately loved Bobby. My mother was anxious to plan a wedding, and at the time I thought it was what I wanted, as well."

"Families sometimes have the best of intentions, but they aren't always right."

"Are you referring to your grandfather?"

Niko nodded. "He sounds a lot like your mother,

except for the part about planning a wedding. That would have never happened."

"Because he believed it's women's work?"

"No. Because it would have taken time away from his work."

"Anyway, when Bobby was home, he was too tired to spend quality time with me. My mother, with her eye on the wedding ring, assured me all was fine. Couples got busy, and we just had to work extra hard to find time to spend together. So I gave up my apartment and moved in with him."

Not that Niko wasn't interested in her background, but he suddenly felt as though this conversation was going much deeper than he'd ever anticipated. The more she opened up to him, the closer they became and the harder it would be for him to keep his distance. "But what does any of this have to do with you wanting a baby at this stage?"

She frowned at him. "I'm getting to it if you'll just give me a minute."

"Sorry." He wasn't. He didn't want to get caught up in her sticky details. He didn't want to empathize with her. He didn't want any entanglements, but he supposed with a baby on the way they would be forever entangled.

"I was certain moving in together would fix things. And it did. At first. Then things fell back into a busy routine. He started working all hours of the day and night, including weekends. It was ridiculous."

"Well, business isn't always conducted between nine and five, you know."

She stopped and planted her hands on her hips. "Who's telling this story?"

Had she really just admonished him? He wasn't used to this. At the office, people cowered in his presence. Not that he'd done anything to warrant such a reaction. He supposed it was the legacy his grandfather had left him. That man had been a force to be reckoned with. His grandfather had made grown men quake in their boots with just a look.

"I was just trying to explain." When Sofia sent him an *Are you done yet?* look, he added, "Okay. Continue."

"Bobby promised it would get better. He said we'd have the rest of our lives together. He just needed some time to work on his career while I cooked, cleaned and did his laundry. He was too busy for those things." She sighed. "This went on for a while, and then I got pregnant. Bobby was excited. We got engaged. He started spending more time at home, and he expected me to be there. He wanted me to quit my job because he thought my place was in the home." Frown lines marred her pretty face. "I refused to quit. I liked getting out of the apartment every day and having my own financial independence."

None of this surprised Niko. Since the first time he met Sofia, she had struck him as fiercely independent. Obviously this story didn't have a happy ending. His gut told him not to push her, that she'd say it when she was ready.

They continued walking. The sea washed up on the shore, ever closer to their feet. The curiosity to know the rest of Sofia's story grew with each roll of the tide.

"And then I lost the baby." A poignant note of pain threaded through her voice. "Bobby didn't say he blamed me, but it was there in his eyes every time he looked at me."

"Don't." Niko stopped her with a gentle hand on her arm. "I don't know anything about pregnancy, but I do know that sometimes in life things happen that are way beyond our control. I'm sure you didn't do anything wrong."

Her gaze met his. "You barely even know me—"

"I know enough."

"And what is it that you think you know about me?"

"That you're an honest person with a good heart who would do anything to protect your child."

Sofia sniffled and blinked repeatedly. "You see a lot."

"Only the truth."

No wonder she was eager to turn her life upside down. He believed she would love their child the way children were supposed to be loved. He was so thankful for that part.

"And your boyfriend, what happened to him? Did he leave you because you wouldn't cave in to his demands?"

"No. But that would have been so much easier."

"Easier than what?"

She shook her head. "Never mind. I shouldn't have rattled on so much."

Just when she was getting to the interesting part, she decided to clam up. Frustration churned in his gut. He wasn't sure if he was more upset with her for stringing him along with her story only to leave him wondering how the jerk had broken her heart, or if he was upset with himself for letting his guard down and caring about her. Maybe it was a bit of both.

"I take that to mean you've sworn off men."

"Yes. And now that I'm pregnant, I don't have time to date. I've got other priorities."

Well, that would make what he had in mind even harder. But he was never one to back down from a challenge. Although the stakes had never been this high.

"Shouldn't you take it easy? You know, after what happened before?" She didn't have to work. He had the resources to keep her comfortable and well cared for throughout her pregnancy.

"I'm fine." She smiled. "I had all of the appropriate tests done, and the doctor doesn't see any reason for the past to repeat itself."

Only then realizing he'd been holding his breath in anticipation of her response, he exhaled. They turned around and started back toward the resort.

Knowing for a fact that she'd oppose any talk of marriage at this point, he was more certain than ever that his plan would work…if only he could convince Sofia to go along with it.

"I have a proposition for you." He didn't know how else to phrase it.

"What sort of proposition?"

"I'd like to hire your services."

She stopped walking and sent him a puzzled stare. "You want to hire me? For what?"

"I'd like you to do some cleaning. I can make it worth your time."

Confusion reflected in her eyes. "Here at the Blue Tide? But I already cleaned your bungalow."

"Let me explain. Tomorrow I leave on a round-the-world trip. The Stravos family over the years has accumulated numerous private residences at a number of the Stravos Star Hotels. It's my job to see they are emptied and cleaned for the new owner."

"I'd like to help you, but I have plans to return to New York."

"I'll take you there at the conclusion of the trip."

She shook her head. "I don't have time for an extended trip. I have to find a home for myself and the baby."

"It'll only be for a few weeks, and I can help you find a place to live." *With me on my private island in Greece*, but he decided to keep that part to himself for now.

"I didn't tell you about the baby so you'd come riding to my rescue. I don't need a knight in shining armor."

"So what are your plans when you return to New York?"

"I'm planning to go back to school."

"School? Really?" By the deepening frown on her face, he'd utterly failed to keep the surprise from his voice.

"It just so happens that I always did well in school."

"So why didn't you get your secondary education?"

She shrugged. "I met my ex just before I graduated high school. And I let myself get distracted, thinking I was in love and trying to make him happy. I always planned to go back someday."

"And this is someday?"

"Yes. I have a knack with numbers, and I intend to get my accounting degree."

"And something tells me you'll do exactly that."

Her admission made him all the more intent on helping her. He couldn't imagine being a single parent would be easy for anyone, especially when the pregnancy was a surprise. And then to go back to school on top of it all.

Luckily he was fast and could think on his feet. He was, after all, a Stravos—his family hadn't amassed a fortune over the years without being quick thinkers and following their guts. He could remedy this by meeting both of their needs.

He turned to her. "Come with me on this trip, and I'll pay the tuition to the school of your choice."

CHAPTER SIX

FOUR YEARS' WORTH of tuition earned in just a few weeks?

Was he for real?

Sofia studied Niko's face, finding a very serious expression there. "Why are you working so hard to get me to agree to this trip?"

"Why not? It's a win-win for both of us. I get help making the suites presentable, and you get money to follow your dreams."

She had to admit that it was tempting—very tempting. But her grandmother had taught her to be suspicious of offers that were too good to be true.

Sofia recalled his earlier admission about not being able to forget their night together. Was he interested in picking up where they'd left off at the wedding? That wasn't going to happen. She wasn't interested in a relationship. She'd been there and done that. Her heart still held the scars. And now with a baby coming, there was no way she was going to risk her heart. Not for Niko. Not for anyone.

"Why me? You can afford to hire anyone."

"Ah...but see, I don't want to spend the next couple of weeks globe-trotting with just anyone. My jet is big but not that big. You and I hit it off. You're entertaining. I like talking to you. And we already know we get along well—"

"That was one night—a night with wine flowing freely. You can't base any decisions on that evening."

"But you do have to admit it was unforgettable."

She glanced away, not about to let him read the truth in her eyes. That night had been amazing—he'd been amazing. But like with all dreams, eventually you woke up and reality settled in. "If I agree, and I'm not saying that I have, but if I did, it'd be purely business."

He inwardly sighed. He'd never had this hard of a time convincing a woman to travel with him. Not about to let her slip through his fingers, he said, "Yes, it'll be business only, if that's what you want."

"It is." And then her eyes twinkled as though a thought had just dawned on her. "And I'd have one other stipulation."

He knew he wasn't going to like this. "And that would be?"

"Your wardrobe."

"What about it?"

"It's not the most practical attire for cleaning out suites. I'm assuming you'll be helping to box up mementos and such." He nodded and she continued, "Then you'll want some more casual clothes. After all, who would do manual labor in a designer suit? Each one probably cost more than a month's rent."

She had a point, and by the frown forming on his face, he couldn't argue. She wondered if he'd ever cleaned and packed up an apartment in his life. His background was so different than hers.

"What are you thinking?"

She shook her head, not about to upset her potential employer. "It's nothing."

"You know you didn't have a problem opening up to me the night of the reception."

"That night was different."

"It'll be a very long trip if we must censor everything we say to each other."

She had to agree. "Fine. I was wondering if you've ever done any cleaning and packing, or if you always had a staff to do it for you."

"It might surprise you to know that at boarding school I was responsible for my half of the dorm room. We learned to do laundry, mop floors, make up our beds and dust. Inspection was every Friday afternoon with some surprise inspections in between."

She struggled to keep her mouth from falling open. Niko Stravos knew how to do laundry? That was more than Bobby ever cared to know. Her ex had expected hot food on the table and clean clothes in the closet without having to lift a helping hand. Niko was way ahead of him.

"I see I've caught you by surprise." His shoulders straightened. "And at the beginning of each semester we were charged with the task of unpacking. When classes concluded, we had to repack all of our belongings. So in answer to your question, yes, I can clean and pack. But I'll need help if I'm going to make good time. And I'm sure you'll do a much better job than me."

Not trusting her judgment after her disastrous relationship with Bobby, she was unsure if Niko was being on the level with her. Not that it mattered. She had a lead on some apartments that would open up in the next month. Her inside source had told her that once they were posted in the paper they'd be snapped up in a New York minute.

"I'm sure you can find someone else to help you." Sofia wasn't giving up her chance to obtain semi-affordable housing, not when her baby was counting on her.

"You're right, I could. But I want you." Niko's tone was firm but not threatening. "And if you know anything about me, you'll know that I generally get what I want. I've already cleared your time off with Cristo—"

"You did what? How could you?" She crossed her arms and glared at him. "You had no right." He'd jeopardized her plans to care for the baby.

"Cristo hinted around that you might not take my butting in well. But he doesn't know the circumstances." Niko combed his fingers through his dark hair, scattering the wavy strands. "I...I thought—"

"You thought wrong. Just because you're richer than Midas and used to getting your way in the boardroom doesn't mean you can bulldoze right over me, my wants and my needs."

"That wasn't what I meant to do."

She lifted her chin. "If you're even considering coparenting with me, you have to learn that

I won't be dictated to. I can make my own decisions, even if they don't always line up with what you want. Is that understood?"

His eyes widened at her outburst, but then he relented and nodded his head. "I understand. Can I at least explain why I made the request on your behalf?"

She'd made her point. Something told her Niko wasn't one to repeat his mistakes. "Go ahead."

"I'm leaving first thing in the morning, and I won't be back for a while. I want you to come with me. I really want your help."

She shook her head. "I can't."

"Is it the baby? Is there something you haven't told me?"

It'd be so easy to tell him that was the case. She gazed up at his face. His forehead was creased with lines, and his eyes had grown dark with worry. She couldn't let him get worked up over a problem that didn't exist—even if it'd make her life easier. No one deserved to needlessly worry about their unborn child.

"The baby is strong and healthy. And there's no reason I can't travel."

"You're sure? Because I don't want to do anything that will jeopardize you or the baby."

Her heart squeezed with his display of concern. No man had ever worried about her like that before—not even her ex when she'd miscarried. Bobby hadn't even made it to the hospital to visit her. And now here was Niko, not even her boyfriend, worried about her.

She quickly tamped down the rush of gratitude because Niko was only worried about the baby—his child—his heir. She meant nothing to him. And it was best that things remained that way. Her heart was already a patchwork of scars. She refused to make it worse.

She swallowed hard. "Yes, I'm sure. The reason I need to get back to New York is that there's an apartment opening up and I want to apply for it."

"I see. Perhaps I could have my PA search for some other apartments and schedule some walk-throughs for you."

"It's more than just the apartment. I have colleges to apply to and day care to line up. Furniture to pick out. Diapers to buy—and the list goes on."

He frowned. "I had no idea. So that's why Cristo didn't think you'd be receptive to my idea."

She shrugged. "Kyra has been cheering me on to go back to school. I wouldn't be surprised if she mentioned it to him."

"So this is something you've been planning, even before you knew about the baby?"

"Yes. I never came to Greece intending to stay forever. The visit was what I needed at the time to get my head back on straight. And now that it is, it's time I go home. I have a list of potential apartments that are in close proximity to my parents, who will most likely volunteer to help with the baby and to lighten my day care expenses. I also need to make a doctor's appointment to get my records up-to-date with the pregnancy."

"You've really done a lot of planning in such a short amount of time. But what about us?"

"Us? There is no us."

The frown lines on his face deepened. "But you're carrying my baby. In my book that makes you and me an us."

"Well, it doesn't to me. We're coparents, nothing more." Wow, was she lying. Even to herself. This baby had forged an unbreakable bond between herself and Niko where one hadn't existed before. Nothing she said was going to erase that. And by the disbelief reflected in Niko's eyes, he wasn't buying what she was saying, either.

Niko's gaze dipped before meeting hers again. "I apologize for overstepping with Cristo and I promise not to do it again so long as you give my proposal due consideration."

"If you really want me to take your offer seriously, you're going to have to be honest with me about why you want me to accompany you on this trip. And, please, don't mention the cleaning thing again. You want something else—I can tell."

Though she wouldn't admit it to him, the college tuition money was truly tempting, especially with a surprise baby on the way. Her savings were rather lacking when she started to think of everything she would need for this new part of her life.

So just how badly did he want her to go on this trip with him?

Was he ready to take the risk and open up to her?

Why did this woman have to question everything he said?

Niko sighed heavily. Something told him that Sofia would stand her ground until she had all the answers. A part of him respected that stubborn streak in her—the trait had just happened to reveal itself at exactly the wrong time.

He thought it over for a moment beneath Sofia's

close scrutiny. She wasn't going to rush him. Let her wait and wonder.

What would it hurt to be perfectly honest with her? After all, she'd been totally up front with him about the baby and why it was so important to her. He really respected her for her honesty and for the fact that she didn't play games with him, which he knew other women might have done to work the situation to their advantage.

"Okay. Here's the deal. I'd like a chance to get to know you better. And with a baby on the way, it seems like the sooner we do that, the better."

She shook her head. "If you have it in your head that you're going to marry me, forget it. I told you before that's not going to happen. I don't need a husband. I can get by on my own."

She may not be interested now, but if he convinced her to go with him, he'd have a couple of weeks to change her mind. He could be persuasive when he set his mind to it. "Are you really prepared to do this all alone, including the three a.m. feedings? The no sleep? The colic? And going to work the next day sleep deprived? I mean, I may not be a parent, but I have plenty of them working for me. And I hear things—sometimes things I'd rather not hear."

After all her bold statements, worry now reflected in her eyes. "You make parenthood sound awful."

And then her eyes grew shiny. She wasn't going to cry, was she? Oh, man, that wasn't what he'd meant to have happen. He was just voicing his concerns out loud. In the future, he'd have to be careful what he said. But for now, he had no clue what to do.

Her eyes shimmered as they met his. There was something about her that got to him more than any other person he'd ever known. She was complicated with the way she was so strong one minute and yet so vulnerable the next. In that moment, he wanted nothing more than to comfort her—to reignite the flame that normally burned so bright in her.

He reached out, brushing the backs of his fingers along her cheek. "Don't worry. We'll figure this all out."

"Are you sure?"

He nodded and hoped he sounded more certain than he felt. "We're in this together."

Her hand reached up and squeezed his. The heat of lingering attraction warmed his veins. With every fiber of his being, he wanted to pull her close and kiss away her fears. His body started to sway toward hers. Just a little farther and they'd be chest to chest. His gaze moved to her glossy lips.

The part of his brain that warned him against such an action was getting drowned out by the pounding of his heart. He knew why they'd had the most amazing night together, and it had absolutely nothing to do with the sparkling wine. It was Sofia. She was simply enchanting with her sunny smile and witty comments that kept him on his toes. He wanted that fun part of her back.

His thumb traced her jawline before brushing over her full bottom lip. There was a rush of intense desire mingled with the excitement of the unknown that had the adrenaline pumping through his veins. He hadn't been this nervous about kissing a girl since high school.

How would she react? The look in her eyes said that she wanted him, too. Or was he just seeing what he wanted to? He glanced down at her very inviting lips. If he were just to lean in and kiss her, he'd wipe away any doubts she might have about them doing what was right for their child. He could make their marriage work for both of them, if only she'd give him a chance.

Questions reflected in her eyes, putting a halt to

his actions. He inwardly groaned as logic wedged its way into his fantasy. As much as he wanted to shove it aside and deal with it later, he couldn't shut off his mind.

The voice of logic said a kiss would be a mistake. He was trying to talk her into taking this trip with him. Where did he think kissing her would lead them? She'd probably turn him down flat, thinking all he wanted was to get lucky. He couldn't let her get the wrong idea about him. He had to show her that he was man enough to keep his hands to himself—for now. Once they were married, well, maybe they could explore their options.

With great reluctance, he pulled his hand away. He took a step back and cleared his throat. "I promise to make this trip as short as possible. And if you're unable to find a suitable apartment, I'll buy a building and become your landlord."

Her mouth gaped. "You're serious, aren't you?"

He nodded. He'd never been more serious in his life. "Come with me. You won't regret it. Besides, it isn't every day you're offered a trip around the world, is it?"

She shook her head. "You promise you'll drop me in New York?"

"You have my word. New York just happens to be on the travel itinerary."

CHAPTER SEVEN

THIS REQUIRED MORE than a text message.

Sofia had arranged to meet Kyra in person to tell her all that had transpired between her and Niko. As the words tumbled from Sofia's mouth one after the other, Kyra's eyes grew round. Sofia hoped her friend would be able to somehow understand that sometimes life happens when you least expect it.

In many ways, Sofia was still coming to terms with all the changes in her life and the knowledge that Niko still made her heart race. She'd have to get over him now that she'd agreed to accompany him on this trip. Their mission was to close the family residences while figuring out how to be good coparents. Anything beyond that would just complicate matters. And right now, they had more than enough complications.

"You're pregnant?" Disbelief echoed in Kyra's voice.

"It might not be the best time or the ideal set of circumstances, but, yes, I'm pregnant."

"And my cousin is the father?"

Sofia nodded as Kyra's mouth gaped. "I think you're in as much shock as he is at the moment."

Kyra didn't say anything for a second. The seconds stretched into a minute and then two. Sofia laced her fingers together to keep from fidgeting. *Please don't be mad.*

Unable to take the extended silence, Sofia asked, "What are you thinking?"

"Do you really want to know?"

Oh, no. Perhaps she didn't want to know. The air caught in Sofia's lungs. Then again, she couldn't stand the suspense. "Just tell me."

"That this makes us officially family." Kyra's face lit up with a smile.

A pent-up breath rushed from Sofia's straining lungs. "Really?"

Kyra nodded as tears of happiness gathered in her eyes before splashing onto her cheeks. "I always thought of us as family, and now it's official."

"Even if I don't marry your cousin? Because you

know about me and men. The two do not mix, at least not for any extended period of time."

"No matter what, you and I are family." They hugged. Kyra pulled back and gave her a serious look. "Now shouldn't you go pack? You have some globe-trotting to do."

For a second there, Sofia had been so wrapped up in worrying about Kyra's reaction that she'd forgotten that come the next morning, she was due to set off on an adventure of a lifetime. "Oh, yes, I should get going."

They hugged again. Her friend pulled back and looked her in the eyes. "Give the guy a chance. You never know what might happen. And I'm not saying that just because he's my cousin."

"Don't get your hopes up." She really hated to disappoint Kyra.

"I won't. But remember what I said."

"I will." Sofia walked away, certain she would keep her guard up around Niko. She couldn't—she wouldn't—be hurt again. Because when the shock of the baby wore off, so would Niko's fascination with her. He would go back to his billionaire lifestyle, and she would return to her conservative life on the Upper East Side. It was the way it had to be.

* * *

This was really happening…

A giddy feeling sent Sofia's stomach fluttering. She was in Tokyo. *Wow!* And here she thought that flying from New York to Greece had been a big deal, but it was nothing compared to a round-the-world trip on a private jet with one of the world's most eligible bachelors. Her heart beat a little faster as the image of Niko came to mind. Right now, he was in the study of the luxury suite dealing with yet another business call.

Sofia took a break from cleaning to stand by a large window that gave an impressive view of the city as the colorful lights dotted the night sky. Talk about being on top of the world. They were fifty floors up in the penthouse suite.

Niko claimed this building was one of the first Stravos Star Hotels, which meant it had been around for quite a while, but you couldn't tell. The lobby of the hotel consisted of glass, white marble and lush potted greenery. It had a grace-ful elegance that made Sofia feel as though she'd stepped into another world—Niko's world.

She'd observed how he'd moved with ease through the building as though it were a sec-ond home for him. It certainly didn't strike her as homey. Everything was updated and modern, from the Oriental artwork adorning the white walls to the computer kiosks off to the side of the lobby. A key card accessed all the hotel's amenities, and there were many, including the very tempting five-star spa. She'd hoped to visit it yesterday after she had finished cleaning for the day, but it was long closed by the time she quit. If only Sofia had a little spare time...

"Sorry about that." Niko returned to the living room, slipping his phone into his pocket. "It was my office in Athens."

She merely nodded, having heard that numerous times already on their trip. She began taping cardboard around a family photo. She had no idea what it was like to be that important, but something told her it wasn't a lot of fun, at least not going by the frown lines that formed on Niko's face every time he pulled the phone out of his pocket.

Needing to finish up the cleaning and packing of the suite, she said, "This is the last of the family portraits. I just need you to tell me if you want any of the artwork on the walls."

"I'm really sorry about leaving you to do the bulk of the work. Yesterday's meetings couldn't be avoided. And today, well, some things cropped up." His lips lowered into a frown. "Why don't you go put up your feet and let me finish?"

She stopped and straightened to look at him. He wanted to do her work? By the look on his face, he was serious. There was no humor to be found in his bottomless gaze. Well, no matter, she didn't shirk her responsibilities.

"You're going to clean in those clothes?" She indicated his blue trousers and light blue dress shirt with the rolled-up sleeves. "You're kidding, right?"

His dark brows furrowed as he glanced down at his clothes. "No worries. I'll be careful."

"Easier said than done. Besides, this is what you hired me to do."

"But I thought we would do everything together."

"Everything?" At the sound of her voice, Niko's eyes glittered with intrigue. Why did she have to vocalize her thoughts?

"Yes. I thought this would be a team effort."

He moved toward her and held out his hand. "Here, let me take that for you."

If he was that insistent, why should she argue? She handed over the scissors and packing tape, then grabbed a fresh rag and dust spray. "Did you spend much time here?"

"Oh, yes. When I was a kid, being this high up was like being on top of the world. But I'm sure you don't want to hear any of that."

"I do." She glanced over her shoulder, pleading with him to continue.

"My grandfather was a busy man. When I was young, he did quite a bit of traveling. If I wasn't away at school, he'd take me with him. In fact, my bedroom is the first one on the right. It's just the way I left it."

"Surely you must have changed it as you grew up." It wasn't until she saw his slightly bemused expression that she realized she'd misspoken.

"Why would I do that?"

Sofia swallowed down her disbelief. "Um, no reason."

Seriously? That was supposed to be his room when he was young? There had been no baseballs or footballs. No posters. No mementos. Nothing like her brothers' rooms had been when they were growing up. Even now, there were still random pieces of their past in their rooms. Their mother never had the heart to remove everything.

But Niko's room was no different than the guest

rooms. No personal mementos. It was so mature. So formal. She couldn't help but wonder if it was indicative of his childhood—proper and stifling.

Niko snipped a piece of tape. "While I waited for my grandfather to get done with his business meetings, I'd read a lot. I had a big imagination."

"I bet that has come in handy."

He ran another strip of tape around the package. "You mean so I could entertain myself? Because you don't have to worry. I always came up with something to do."

"No, that wasn't what I meant." The sad image of him as a little boy in this big suite with no other kids around filled her mind. Her heart went out to him for having to find ways to constantly entertain himself. She'd never had that problem with all her brothers and cousins around. "I meant now that you are the boss, you can use your imagination to envision a big, bright future for the company."

He nodded in understanding. "I have lots of plans for the Stravos Trust. I just wish my ideas didn't meet so much resistance."

"Well, you did just take over, didn't you?"

"I've been working there in one manner or another most of my life."

"Really?" She stopped dusting a gold Oriental table with hand painted bamboo, pink flowers and hummingbirds on the front. "You worked there as a kid."

Niko moved the now-packaged portrait and leaned it against the wall with the others that were being shipped back to Greece. "I didn't have a full-time position, if that's what you mean. But I was being groomed to assume control of the company one day."

"Wouldn't you have rather been outside playing with your friends?"

He shrugged. "I didn't have many friends, just a few I made at boarding school. I didn't have time to hang out. I had my studies to concentrate on."

"So you were always an overachiever?"

He shrugged. "There were expectations I had to meet. As a Stravos, I was expected to live up to my father's memory. I had to be the best in my class. Second best wasn't good enough for a Stravos."

"Niko, I'm so sorry. That must have been so difficult for you."

He shrugged. "It was no different from how my father and grandfather were raised."

"Oh." She wasn't sure what to say at that point, not wanting to upset him.

"You have to understand that the Stravos Trust has far-reaching interests. It's not a job one can just step into. It takes years to learn how it all comes together. And without my father to take his rightful place at the helm, it has become my responsibility."

That was such a big burden to place on such young shoulders. She wondered if Niko ever got to be a kid. Surely he wouldn't want the same thing for their child. Without thinking, she gently touched her stomach.

"What's the matter?" Concern laced Niko's voice. "Are you feeling all right?"

Sofia jerked her hand away from her midsection. She wasn't about to admit the direction of her thoughts. Not at this point. Niko hadn't even discussed custody with her. "I'm fine."

"Maybe you should rest." He moved to her side, and, without giving her a chance to protest, he took the rag from her hand.

"Hey!"

He held the cloth out of her reach. Considering he had quite a few inches on her, it didn't take much. "Go rest. I've got this."

With this being the last room that needed to be dusted and vacuumed, she wasn't going to fight with him. Her knees were sore from kneeling, and her back ached from bending over. But the suite was clean and had the fresh scent she always enjoyed.

She admired the way he got to work. When his phone rang, he ignored it. She could hardly believe her eyes as he forwarded it to voice mail. "If you need to take that, I can finish."

"I told you I've got this. I'll return the call later."

A few minutes of awkward silence passed before Sofia spoke. "How soon are we leaving?"

"We're staying here tonight, and tomorrow we'll take off."

"Oh." She had to admit that she was bummed they wouldn't be sticking around Tokyo long enough for her to go exploring. She'd seen a bit of it on their way to the Stravos Star Hotel, but not nearly enough. She hoped Niko would slow down at some of their stops for her to do some sightseeing. "You were able to take care of all your business here so quickly?"

He nodded. "Mission accomplished, and I found the first piece of the puzzle."

"Puzzle? You make it sound like you're on some sort of scavenger hunt."

"I am, in a manner of speaking."

"That sounds awfully intriguing. If you don't mind me asking, what are you searching for?"

He hesitated. "It's nothing. I shouldn't have mentioned it."

"I'm glad you did. After all, I thought part of the reason you invited me along on this trip was so we could get to know each other better since we're going to be coparenting."

"Yes, you're right." He left the room and quickly returned carrying a folder. He withdrew a paper from the manila folder and handed it to her. "Here. This will explain things better than I ever could."

Her questioning gaze moved from his drawn face to the paper in his hand. There was handwriting all over it as though it were a letter. She was reluctant at first to take it. She had the distinct feeling Niko wouldn't have so readily shared his motives if it weren't for her prodding. Words of refusal teetered on her tongue.

"Go ahead. Take it." He continued holding the paper out to her.

She accepted it, even though she wasn't comfortable with the situation. She'd just wanted him to open up a bit and let her in. She didn't mean to make him feel obligated to her. This getting-to-know-each-other stuff was going to be much harder than she'd ever imagined.

She glanced down at the distinct handwriting with strong strokes. Niko's name was at the top. Her questioning gaze met Niko's once more to see if he'd changed his mind before she went further. When he nodded, she turned back to the letter, quite unsure what she would learn.

Niko,

I know that I was not the replacement father you deserved. By the time you knew me, I was an old man who was quite set in my ways. It wasn't always this way. Perhaps you were too young to remember the adventures your father would lead us on. And that is my fault. Instead of keeping those memories alive for you, it was easier and less painful not to speak of them. And so before this deal is finalized with Cristo Kiriakas, I am sending you on a very important mission. You are to visit and close the family's apartments in each of the following hotels: Tokyo, Honolulu, New Orleans, the Caribbean and New York City.

Most of what you'll find will be of no value to you and can be disposed of quickly. But in each apartment is a safe. In them, you will find pieces of your past. Things I should have given you years ago. Forgive this old man for his procrastination.

If I should die before you complete the mission, the Stravos Trust will be yours to do with as you see fit. But I beg you to do as I ask. Though I taught you everything I know about business, there are other life lessons that I failed to impart to you. This is my attempt to set things right.

Now go with an open mind and heart. And know that I love you.
Bon Voyage

She wasn't sure what to say to Niko now. He was truly on a sort of real-life scavenger hunt. She glanced over at him. They were so close and yet so far away. She was beginning to see him with new eyes—a lonely little boy who'd lost his parents and was forgotten by a driven grandfather. Her heart went out to him.

When Niko glanced up, catching her gaze, she knew she had to say something—anything to make this moment less awkward. "So our next stop is Hawaii?"

"It is. How does that sound to you?"

"Wonderful." A smile tugged at her lips. "I've always wanted to go there."

"Then your wish is my command."

If only...

Her mind skidded off in a totally inappropriate direction... Niko would sweep her into his arms. His lips would claim hers. The daydream sent her heart racing. Her gaze landed on the man of her dreams, admiring his broad shoulders, narrow waist and firm backside. He was definitely worthy of a dream or two.

A sigh passed by her lips. Too bad that's all it'd ever be.

CHAPTER EIGHT

AT LAST THE jet began a slow descent as they neared the Hawaiian Islands. Niko glanced over to find Sofia napping in her seat. He wished she had taken him up on his earlier suggestion for her to go curl up in the bed at the rear of the plane. She'd have been so much more comfortable.

As it was, her head lolled to the side and her arms were wrapped tightly about her as though she was cold. He supposed that was possible because he liked to keep the thermostat on the cooler side. He grabbed his suit jacket and got to his feet.

With the utmost care, he draped it over her. She murmured something he couldn't make out, but she never fully woke up. He wouldn't rouse her until he absolutely had to. It was obvious she'd worn herself out cleaning the suite in Tokyo. He admonished himself once again for not doing more to help her.

As he stood in front of her, he couldn't help but notice her unique beauty. He longed to reach out

JENNIFER FAYE   103

and stroke her creamy complexion. If their baby took after her, it would be aces in the looks department. It was still so unreal to him that she was carrying his baby.

Quietly he made it back to his seat and picked up his computer, but he couldn't stop thinking of Sofia and their baby. In what? Six months or so, there'd be a new Stravos in this world. And long before then he intended to take Sofia as his bride. The more time he spent with her, the more certain he became that this was the right decision for all three of them.

He forced himself to stare at the computer monitor, but he found himself unable to concentrate on analyzing the figures on his screen. His gaze blurred. He rubbed his tired eyes. With a sigh, he closed the computer. These long hours working were starting to catch up to him.

A green folder sticking out of his briefcase drew his attention. It was what he'd retrieved from the wall safe in the Tokyo penthouse. He'd been distracted by helping Sofia move furniture in order to clean and had put off investigating the file's contents. What could be so important that his grandfather had sent him on this round-the-world journey?

Niko withdrew the expandable folder from his briefcase. He reached inside and pulled out a stack of black-and-white photos.

"What in the world?"

He hadn't meant to speak the words out loud. His surprised reaction had Sofia shifting in her seat. He pressed his lips together, waiting and hoping she'd doze off again. When he didn't hear anything further, he continued his search.

One by one he examined the photos for a sign of someone he recognized. But none of the faces looked familiar. When he turned the photos over, he found names and dates. These people—these strangers—were his family.

Sofia yawned and stretched her arms above her head, letting his jacket slide down over her gentle curves and gather in her lap. "Whatcha doing?"

He glanced over at her. Her short dark hair was mussed, and her cheeks were rosy from her nap. Her smile made her eyes sparkle like gemstones. She looked absolutely adorable. An unfamiliar sensation swirled within him and settled in his chest, filling him with warmth.

"Niko? Is everything all right?"

"Hmm? Oh, yes. I was just looking at some old photos."

"Is that what your grandfather left you in the safe in Tokyo?"

Niko nodded. "Except I don't know any of these people. I mean, I know that I'm somehow related to them, but they don't mean anything to me." Frustrated with whatever lesson his grandfather was trying to teach him, he tossed them back in the folder. "I knew this trip was going to be one big waste of time. And this just proves it."

"May I see the photos?"

"Sure." He handed over the folder and got to his feet. "They're of no value to me."

"Of no value? How can you say that? These people are your family."

He shook his head. "They are people I never met, never knew. They mean nothing to me."

A frown flickered across her face, but she didn't say anything as she removed one photo after the next. "How can this not mean anything to you? Most people want to know about their past. Look at your cousin, Kyra. She traveled half the globe in the hopes of finding some part of her past."

"I'm not like that. I'm fine just the way I am. I don't need some old photos to make me feel whole."

"But don't you ever wonder where you got

your dark, wavy hair? Or perhaps your blue-gray eyes?"

He shook his head. "I look like my grandfather. But who cares?"

"Perhaps your son or daughter will care? Won't you want to be able to tell them about their family?"

He hadn't considered that. "I don't know what I'd tell them."

"Perhaps that's what your grandfather is trying to do for you—give you some answers. Maybe there are questions you never thought of asking. And maybe right now these photos don't mean anything to you, but once you're a father, the past and the future will collide. It will mean something to you then."

"Perhaps you're right."

His gut told him his grandfather would have approved of Sofia. She might like to have a good time now and then, but she had a level head on her shoulders. And perhaps she would have understood his grandfather in ways that Niko was never able to grasp.

If Sofia was right, at least this trip wouldn't be a total waste of time. He still couldn't help but wonder why he had to travel from country to country collecting these photos. It made no sense to him when his grandfather could have gathered it all and left everything in a box at the house on their private island.

But what puzzled Niko the most was the fact that his grandfather wasn't one to send him on a fool's errand. There had to be more to this trip than he'd figured out so far. What could it be?

Niko got to his feet and moved about the plane, stretching his aching muscles. Some people may think that a round-the-world trip was something dreams were made of, but not him—not with the frantic pace that he planned to complete this trip. The sooner it was done, the sooner he'd have a clear conscience—having fulfilled his grandfather's final wish.

And then Niko could concentrate fully on his plans to expand the shipping segment of the Stravos Trust. He already had the construction of his first megacargo carrier under way.

When his phone buzzed, he answered it. After he hung up, he turned to Sofia. "That was the pilot. He said to buckle up. We're getting ready to land in Honolulu."

She set aside his jacket and strapped in. "I've never been to Hawaii. Will we be here long?"

"Long enough to close up the suite."

"Oh." She didn't expand on her disappointment, but it was quite evident in her tone.

He hadn't thought about her expectations when he'd invited her on this trip. Perhaps he should have done a better job of explaining his aggressive agenda. She was probably imagining a leisurely trip where she'd get to relax and take in the sights.

He inwardly groaned. The last thing in the world he wanted to do now was play tourist. But it wasn't fair of him to keep her prisoner on this jet as it spanned the world. "Would you like to do some sightseeing?"

"Yes." Her answer came quickly, but then she pressed her lips together as though realizing she shouldn't have shown her eagerness so readily. "I mean, it's okay if you're too busy and don't have time. I'd understand."

He didn't want to, but he would make time to spend one day sightseeing. After all, there was no reason they couldn't fly at night. "Then it's decided. We'll go sightseeing. Anything special you want to see?"

"Um...everything." Her eyes lit up like his employees' when Christmas bonuses were hand delivered by him.

"That's a lot. I'm not sure we have time to squeeze in everything. But if you make a list, we'll work on it."

"Okay."

"Why don't you hand me those?" He gestured to the photos. "They aren't much to look at."

She glanced down at the stack of photos all in different shapes and sizes. "I'm surprised you never saw any of these before. You mean you didn't have any copies at your house in Greece?" When he shook his head, she added, "How strange."

"Not necessarily." He didn't want to admit it, but he had given the photos some consideration. "Can I see a few of them?"

She scooped up half the stack and handed them to him. He started flipping through them one at a time. But this time, instead of focusing on the people, he studied the background. And in almost every photo he was able to identify a location in Tokyo. "I think all of these were taken someplace in Tokyo. The penthouse must have been open to the extended family's use. So it's only natural that some photos would gather there over time."

"You should have them put in a scrapbook."

"Why would I do that?"

"To keep them nice and make it easy for you to look over them from time to time."

She obviously had much stronger family ties than he'd ever had in his life. "Is that what you do with your photos, place them in scrapbooks?"

She nodded. "My mother loves to make them. She took a class at a local craft store and now she makes fancy scrapbooks with colorful paper and stickers. She uses all sorts of things. They're so popular that family members are always asking her to make one for them for various occasions like weddings, baby showers and graduations."

He'd never had anyone care enough about the details of his life to want to paste them in a book. He didn't even have a clue if his grandfather had any snapshots of him as a kid other than the formal portraits that hung in the living room. "That must be a very special gift."

"It is. I'm sure when I return to New York that my mother will be following me around with her camera. She's going to be so excited about her first grandchild."

"Is that what you truly want—to return to New York?"

Sofia nodded. "I want to be with my family when the baby is born."

And he wasn't family. She didn't say it, but she didn't have to. He could hear the unspoken words loud and clear. Once again he was on the outside looking in. His grandfather did the best he could for him, but he was older and had no patience for an overactive young boy.

And now once again, Niko should be a part of a family, but instead he was left on the fringes. He clenched his hands. Why did he feel as if he had to work for a place in this new family? Weren't those sorts of things supposed to come naturally without so much effort?

No matter what, he wasn't giving up. He didn't want his son or daughter growing up like he had, wondering about his parents and what they'd been like.

Niko looked down at the photos. His problem was that he was thinking about Sofia and this baby too much. Everything would work out just as it should. He always got what he went after— some things just took more patience than others.

His gaze strayed back to Sofia. He was going to need lots of patience. His attention zeroed in on her glossy lips. And lots of restraint—until they said, *I do.*

So this was Hawaii?

Sofia smiled as she glanced around from the balcony of their penthouse suite in Honolulu. A warm breeze rushed over her skin. She couldn't imagine why Niko would ever want to part with such an amazing view. Blue skies overhead were dotted by small puffy white clouds. She looked down at Waikiki Beach. This place was like heaven on earth with the white sand and clear water. So much like the Blue Tide Resort and yet so different.

Niko had been gone by the time she woke up that morning. Her nap on the plane just hadn't been relaxing, and she had been wiped out by the time they reached Niko's penthouse suite in the Stravos Star Hotel.

They'd agreed to a good night's sleep before sightseeing the next day. So when she awoke and found herself alone in the suite, she was surprised. On the kitchen counter, she found a note with her name on it.

I'll be back by noon. There's food in the refrigerator or feel free to ring room service. See you soon, Niko

She glanced at her watch. It was half past twelve, and she was anxious to get out and enjoy her one day in Hawaii. She was already frustrated that she'd slept so late. Time was ticking away.

Just then her phone buzzed. She rushed over to the table by the wall of windows, hoping it was Niko. Which she knew was crazy. It wasn't as if they were here on vacation or anything. But she couldn't help missing him just a little.

When she clicked on her phone, there was a text message from Kyra.

Mop&Glow007 (Kyra): Just thinking about you. What part of the world are you in now?

MaidintheShade347 (Sofia): Hawaii. It's gorgeous.

Mop&Glow007 (Kyra): Am totally jealous.

MaidintheShade347 (Sofia): You're in sunny Greece. You can't be jealous.

Mop&Glow007 (Kyra): Says who? A trip around the world sounds amazing.

It would be if the situation was different. Niko hadn't invited her along because he was interested in picking up where they'd left off. No, he was busy trying to decide what he wanted to do about the baby. She knew he had enough money and influence to cause problems for her regarding custody. She couldn't give him any reason to think the baby wouldn't be well cared for with her.

Her phone chimed again, drawing her from her thoughts. She glanced down to find another message from Kyra.

Mop&Glow007 (Kyra): Am I to assume you and Niko have hit it off?

Seconds turned to minutes as Sofia contemplated the question. She knew what Kyra meant—that they'd hooked up romantically. That ship had sailed. Right now, they were concentrating on becoming friends. And she'd give Niko credit, when he wasn't on the phone or computer, he made conversation. The problem was sometimes she wished they'd do more than just talk—

Chime. Chime. Chime.

Mop&Glow007 (Kyra): Sofia? You still there?

MaidintheShade347 (Sofia): Sorry. I'm here. We're okay.

Mop&Glow007 (Kyra): Okay? That's not very encouraging.

Sofia didn't know what to say to that. Perhaps Kyra wasn't the best person to confide in about her complicated relationship with Niko. After all, he was Kyra's cousin and they'd just been recently united. Sofia didn't want to do anything to hamper that new relationship.

MaidintheShade347 (Sofia): Everything is good. No worries. I'm just heading out now.

Mop&Glow007 (Kyra): Oh, good. I was starting to worry.

MaidintheShade347 (Sofia): Well, stop. I'll message later.

Mop&Glow007 (Kyra): Hugs.

MaidintheShade347 (Sofia): Hugs back.

Sofia really missed her best friend. But this was one situation where she would have to work through it on her own. The truth was even if Kyra were here in Hawaii with her, there was no way she'd tell her about the kisses she'd shared with Kyra's cousin or the looks that had passed between herself and Niko. Kyra would jump to the wrong conclusion, thinking there was hope for a happily-ever-after.

The truth of the matter was that aside from chemistry, they had nothing in common…except the baby. Once she showed him she was fully capable of taking care of herself, he'd stop worrying and go back to his business, letting her raise the baby in peace. Or at least she hoped so.

And she'd start by getting out of this suite and showing herself around Honolulu. She didn't need Niko to play tour guide. She would do fine on her own.

She grabbed her phone and bag. After jotting a note to Niko, she headed out the door. She rushed to the elevator, taking it down to the ground floor. The lobby of the Stravos Star Hotel was congested. Sofia glanced around, hoping to catch sight of Niko, but she didn't see anyone that even remotely resembled his tall, dark good looks.

With a shrug, she refused to be disappointed. After all, she had an adventure awaiting her. And photos to take as she'd promised to send some to her mother and Kyra. She would have a good time…and for just a little bit, she'd stop worrying about the future.

She stepped outside and immediately squinted in the bright sunshine. She slipped on her sunglasses and started off toward the beach. A stroll along the shore with the water washing over her feet would be just what she needed to soothe away the tension that had the muscles in her body stiff and sore.

She paused at the edge of the patio area and gazed out at the crowd of people littering the beach. There were older people, younger people, little kids and lifeguards. But what caught and held her attention was the large number of couples. Some were sitting side by side reading. Others were playing and laughing. And then others were walking hand in hand.

It was at that particular moment that Sofia felt a poignant stab of loneliness. She would never have that closeness because she refused to accept anything less than true love. The kind that came with promises of devotion, undying love and forever. The kind of relationship her parents and grandparents had found. And that sort of love seemed impossible for her to find.

Her thoughts tripped back to Bobby and how he'd said all the right words. Then when things got serious, he expected her to be the little lady waiting on him hand and foot. He didn't respect her work outside the home and that hurt—a lot.

When she'd become pregnant that seemed to help for a bit. Everything was the baby this or the baby that...until she'd miscarried. Bobby had soon become uninterested in her. She wouldn't let the same thing happen with Niko. If she let another man into her life, it'd be because he cared about her and not the fact that she was carrying his child. She needed to be loved for herself.

She approached the concrete steps leading to the sandy beach and started down them. And then she heard something. Was someone calling her name? Niko? Her heart picked up its pace. Had he taken time out of his busy day to be with her?

When she went to turn around, her foot missed the step. She reached out for the rail, but she was too far away. A scream tore from her lungs. Her body lurched forward.

Panic had her mind freezing up. Her body smacked the concrete. In a blur, she tumbled down the set of steps. She landed at the bottom in a heap.

CHAPTER NINE

"SOFIA!"

Niko sprinted toward her. His dress shoes pounded the stone patio. He dodged tables, chairs and loitering people. *Please. No. Let her be okay.*

But he'd been too far away. He could do nothing more than watch her lose her balance and topple down the steps. His chest tightened. By the time he reached the top of the steps, she was lying at the bottom.

He took the steps two at a time. When he reached her side, she was attempting to sit up. There was blood smudged from her lip onto her chin. Angry brush burns marred her beautiful complexion.

"Sofia, it's okay. I'm here."

"I...I'm fine. I, um, just need to get up."

He pressed a gentle hand to her shoulder. "Don't move. You aren't fine. You're bleeding."

"I am?" She moved her hand in front of her and stared at the blood on her palm. Her voice rose to an eerie, shrill level. "The baby." Her hand pressed to her abdomen, smearing blood over her top.

Niko swallowed hard. *Please don't let her lose the baby.* He slipped out his phone and with shaky fingers dialed 9-1-1. He gave the operator the necessary information, including the fact Sofia was pregnant.

"Niko, do you think that's necessary?" Sofia's eyes widened with worry.

Though he was fully concerned as she'd taken quite a tumble, he couldn't let on to her that he was anything but calm and positive. "It's just a precaution. Where's the pain?"

"I...I don't know. It hurts all over."

He wasn't a doctor, but he'd hazard a guess she was experiencing a bit of shock. "Don't worry. The hospital will get you all checked out and cleaned up."

A few tense moments passed as a rather large crowd of curious onlookers had formed around them. Sofia glanced up hesitantly. And then she tried once again to get to her feet. "I need to move. Everyone's staring."

Niko again placed his hand on her shoulder. "What you need to do is stay still. You and the baby had quite a fall. Just rest." He got to his feet, but he didn't move from her side. He assumed his boardroom demeanor, hoping these people would take him as seriously as the board did when he used his no-nonsense tone. "Thank you for your concern. We have everything under control. Please move on and give the young woman some space."

Thankfully most of the people walked away, leaving just a few looky-loos here and there. At least they weren't breathing down their necks. Niko kneeled down next to Sofia. Her face was pale, and her eyes were filled with unshed tears. *Not a good sign. Not good at all. Where's that ambulance?*

"Hey there, how are you doing?"

"I...I'm scared. What if—"

"Shh...don't think about what-ifs. Just think positive. This will all work out."

"But if—"

"You and the baby will be fine." He hoped he sounded more certain than he felt at the moment. A commotion at the top of the steps had Niko glancing up to find the paramedics rushing toward them. "See. Help is here. You'll be all fixed up in no time."

"And the baby?"

Niko squeezed her hand. "The baby will be fine." He glanced up at the paramedic. "She's pregnant."

The man nodded in understanding. "How far along?"

Niko thought back to the wedding and how beautiful Sofia had looked. "It'll be fourteen weeks on Saturday."

Surprise flickered in the paramedic's eyes, but he didn't ask how Niko could be so exact about the date of conception, and Niko was relieved. He didn't want to delve into his very complicated relationship with Sofia. He wouldn't know what to say or how to explain the flurry of emotions she created within him.

He stepped back just enough for the two paramedics to treat her. But Niko didn't go far. He would be right there making sure Sofia got the treatment she needed. And in case she called out for him, he wanted to be there for her.

After all, this was all his fault. If he hadn't been so anxious to catch up to her—if he hadn't called out her name—she wouldn't have turned around, and her foot wouldn't have missed the step. He cursed his own stupidity. What had he done?

All morning the meetings with the hotel staff had dragged on. One after the other with no end in sight, and all he could think about was Sofia. He'd wanted to slip away and head straight for the penthouse, but questions from his staff kept cropping up.

Never in his life had he been torn between his private life and that of his business. It had to be the news of the baby—that had to be it. Because he was immune to love. Niko was smarter than to get caught up in something that wouldn't last.

But if he was so smart, then why had he put the mother of his child in such peril? He thanked his lucky stars that Sofia appeared to be all right, but questions still remained where the baby was concerned. And that was all on him.

He continued to stare at Sofia, seeing the fear reflected in her eyes. And he knew she wasn't worried about herself. She was scared of losing her baby—their baby.

In that moment, he knew he'd sacrifice anything to make this right for her.

Poked, prodded and bandaged.

Sofia lay on the hospital gurney. She fidgeted with the edge of the bleached white sheet.

They'd been anxiously awaiting the doctor for what felt like forever. What was taking so long? She glanced at Niko as he paced back and forth within the small exam room as though he were a caged animal. He was probably thinking she was totally irresponsible. And he'd be right. She had only one important job to do right now—take care of their baby. And she'd failed miserably.

The baby just had to be okay. Sofia would never be able to forgive herself if her carelessness had hurt her child. The memory of her miscarriage and that sense of emptiness plagued her. She couldn't go through that again. She'd do anything to keep the baby safe. She sent up a silent prayer.

She blinked repeatedly, willing her emotions to remain under wraps. The only thing that could make this situation worse was for her to break down in tears. She glanced over at Niko. His head was lowered and his shoulders drooped as he paced the length of the private room.

She should say something to make him feel better, but no words would come. All she could think about was the baby and willing it to be okay. Did that make her selfish? Thoughtless?

And then, unable to stand the sound of his dress

shoes clicking over the tiled floor, she uttered, "You don't have to stay."

Niko stopped pacing and turned to her. His handsome face was creased with lines. "I'm not going anywhere, not until I know that you and the baby are all right."

"What if…" Her shaky voice trailed away. She squeezed her eyes shut. How could she have been so clumsy?

Niko sat on the edge of her bed and stared deep into her eyes. "Think positive."

"But what if—"

"Everything will be fine." He reached out, running his hand down over her hair and stroking her cheek.

His fingers moved over a tender spot on her jaw, but she didn't say anything. Right now every part of her was sore. She definitely wouldn't recommend tumbling down steps to anyone. But somehow with Niko sitting there next to her, her aches lessened to some extent.

Was it wrong that she took comfort in his touch when her own child was at risk? And why should his soothing words bring her such peace? There was definitely something special about Niko that went so much deeper than his good looks. There was a tender, caring side of him that she was just getting to see, and she'd like to see so much more of it.

"Maybe you're right." She tried to send him a reassuring smile, but she just couldn't muster the expression. Though she was no longer on the verge of tears, she was still a ball of nerves. "I haven't had any cramping in a while now. Not since the nurse was here." Sitting in this small room with no clock and no window made it impossible for her to tell how much time had passed. "How long has that been?"

Niko consulted his Rolex watch. "I'd say at least thirty minutes."

"Seems more like forever. But the lack of cramping must be a good sign." She rubbed her hand over her abdomen. "You just stay in there, little one. It's not time for you to make an appearance yet."

"See, there you go. Thinking positive is always helpful."

And then out of the blue, a worrisome thought struck her. Would Niko think that if she couldn't take care of herself, she couldn't take care of the baby? She studied him as though by staring at him long enough and hard enough, she'd gain insight into his thoughts. Maybe if she explained—apologized—he wouldn't make a big deal of this.

"Niko, it was an accident. I didn't mean to—"

The door swung open, and the doctor strode in wearing a white lab coat. She'd previously examined Sofia and had decided that a sonogram was in order. "How are you feeling? Is the cramping decreasing?"

Sofia gave her answer some thought, trying to remember what the cramps had felt like when she'd first arrived at the ER. "Yes."

"But you're still experiencing some cramping?"

"Not for a while now. At least a half hour."

"Good. Let's have a look at your baby. Would you like that?"

"Yes." But it wasn't Sofia that responded. It was Niko.

The doctor glanced over at Niko. "Are you the baby's father?"

"Yes. I'm Niko Stravos." He shook hands with the doctor. "I can step outside."

He started for the door. Sofia decided it was silly. He had every reason to stay here and be reassured their baby was safe and unharmed. "Niko, stay. You can see the baby for the first time with me."

His dark brows rose in surprise. "You're sure?"

"I am."

He moved to the opposite side of the bed. He stood a couple of feet away from her. It was as though there was a wall standing between them. How had they gone from laughing, flirting and making love to now being awkward parents?

Sofia's hands grew cold and clammy as she anxiously waited to see with her own eyes that her baby was all right. It seemed like an eternity until the doctor had the image up on the monitor. At first there was no sound. *How can that be? Please let there be a heartbeat.*

The doctor moved the probe around a bit more. And then a smile lit up the doctor's face. She turned the monitor toward Sofia and pointed. "See. Right there is your baby."

The doctor flicked on a switch, and the *swish-swish* of the baby's heart filled the room, bringing tears of joy to Sofia's eyes. *Thank goodness.*

She choked down the rush of emotion. "Is...is it all right?"

"Your baby appears quite strong and healthy. A lot like its mother."

Sofia blew out a pent-up breath. It wasn't until Niko took her hand in his that she remembered he was still by her side. She glanced up at him and saw undeniable happiness.

She squeezed his hand. No words were needed. They were both thinking the same thing. Their baby was safe. It was just a simple gesture—the joining of hands—but the warmth of his touch soothed something deep inside her. In the strength of his grasp, she received a boost to her flagging courage. And in his eyes, she found a depth she hadn't noticed before.

Her heart *tip-tap-tapped* in her chest, and she quickly glanced away. When she tried to pull her hand away, hoping to get her common sense back, he didn't let go. What did this mean? Was he just relieved about the baby's welfare? Or was there something more?

"Do you know if it's a boy or a girl?" Sofia couldn't help but be curious. She wanted every snippet of information she could get about the baby.

"I'm afraid it's too soon for that."

After printing out two photos for them, one for her and one for him, the doctor turned to them. "We're going to keep you here for a bit longer."

"Is there something wrong?"

"No. I just want to make sure the cramping

doesn't return. As soon as it's safe, I'm going to send you home, where I'm sure you'll rest better. The thing is I want you to stay off your feet and give this little one some rest. You both went through quite an ordeal today."

"You mean bed rest?" Niko spoke up.

"Yes, will that be a problem?"

"No."

"Yes."

Niko and Sofia spoke overtop each other. The doctor got a perplexed look on her face. Sofia glanced at Niko, wondering why he'd said no.

"We're traveling," Sofia explained. "The day after tomorrow we're taking off for the mainland."

Niko shook his head. "There's no reason we can't remain here, especially if it's best for Sofia and the baby."

"But you need to go on without me—"

Niko frowned at her. "Stop worrying. You heard the doctor. You can put your feet up, and I'll wait on you."

Was he serious? He was talking as if he were the one who'd fallen and hit his head. He was going to take care of her? She glanced down at their clasped hands, and her pulse raced. She was in his hands both literally and figuratively.

"Good. I'm glad to hear it's all taken care of." The doctor's gaze moved from Niko to Sofia. "I know it's tempting to rush back to your normal routine as soon as you're feeling better, but give it a little time. You had what could have been a serious fall today, and you got lucky. I want to see you in a week for a follow-up."

"A week?" She couldn't be that much of an imposition to Niko. She knew how much he needed to finish this trip and get back to work. "Could I fly back to New York and rest there?"

The doctor moved to the door. "I'd rather you didn't. Not yet. Besides, when you wake up tomorrow, you're going to be awfully sore. You'll be glad to stay put for a while."

"She'll be fine." Niko spoke up. "I promise to have her back for her follow-up."

"But I need to get back to New York—"

"And I'll take you as soon as you're ready."

"But what about your trip—your mission? It's important." Worry filled her eyes. "Promise me you'll see it through to the end."

He hesitated. "If you promise to follow the doctor's orders."

"I do."

"Good." The doctor smiled. "The nurse will be

in with all of the follow-up information. But if you have any problems between now and then, don't hesitate to call my office or come back to the ER."

Once the doctor was gone and they were alone, Niko withdrew his hand from hers and walked to the other side of the exam room. Sofia clenched her fingers, still feeling the lingering heat from his touch. She struggled to keep from frowning.

"You don't have to do this." She wanted to give him an out. She was certain he wasn't the least bit thrilled with having to take care of her, not when he had more important things requiring his attention.

Niko continued to stare at the picture of their baby. "I said I would look after you, and I meant it."

"But I don't want you doing it out of obligation."

His head lifted and his gaze met hers, but she was unable to read his thoughts. "Why shouldn't I feel obligated? You're in Hawaii because of me. The baby you are carrying is mine. And the reason you fell is because of me. I'm taking care of you. End of story."

Really? That's what he thought? He was taking responsibility for her accident instead of blaming her. She struggled to keep her mouth from gaping. This man standing before her was much more complicated than she'd first assumed, and it made her all the more anxious to get to know him better—for the baby's sake, of course.

CHAPTER TEN

CHAPTER TEN

EVERYTHING WILL BE all right.

Niko assured himself as he once again checked on Sofia. She looked so peaceful napping in the master bedroom of the suite at the Honolulu Stravos Star Hotel. It'd been twenty-four hours since the accident, and so far there hadn't been any setbacks. It just had to stay that way.

He returned to the spacious living room and settled in a black leather chair behind a rustic mango wood desk. It wasn't nearly as big as his desk back in Athens, but it would do. A gentle breeze blowing in off the ocean sent the sheer white curtains in the living room rustling.

Niko stared at the monitor, watching the number of unread emails mounting with each passing minute. Something big was going down with one of the assets Niko was interested in purchasing. It was so frustrating to be halfway around the world from the action. He should be in the office leading the charge to fend off this takeover attempt.

Instead his highly qualified, highly paid executives were handling the situation.

He wasn't used to being on the sidelines. His usual spot was in the thick of things. Under any other circumstances, he'd already be jetting back to Athens. But these were extraordinary circumstances to say the least.

He'd had no idea how much this baby meant to him until Sofia's accident. Once he'd known she would be okay, all he could do was will their baby to hang in there. And now not even an emergency at the office could drag him away from Sofia's side. He had to trust that the people working for him would do what needed to be done.

Niko pushed away from the desk. The chair wheels rolled quietly over the wooden floor. He got to his feet and strode to the open doors leading to the veranda, needing a breath of fresh air. Being on the top floor of the Stravos Star Hotel gave him an unobstructed view of Diamond Head. He leaned back against the door frame and focused on the scenery, hoping it'd relax him.

He remembered as a kid wanting to climb Diamond Head, but his grandfather was always too busy. Niko had been left in the care of nannies— boring ones who preferred to watch their soap operas rather than entertain an energetic boy. Instead, he'd gotten into his own mischief in the hotel. His grandfather hadn't been amused, at all.

Niko recalled numerous times being chased through the hallways by the bellman. What was his name? It'd been so long since he'd recalled these memories that they were a bit hazy.

After a moment, it came to him. Mr. Kalama. How could he have forgotten that tall, lanky man, who wore the most serious expression? Niko didn't think he'd ever seen the man smile. It just made it all the more tempting to play harmless pranks on him, such as hanging out-of-order signs on all the elevators and forcing the man to take the steps. Or moving the wet-paint sign. But the thing Niko remembered most was when he ended up being caught in his pranks. Mr. Kalama would give chase. It was the most entertainment Niko had while traveling with his grandfather.

"And what has you smiling?" Sofia's gentle voice filled the room.

He was smiling? He glanced over at Sofia. Today her bruises had become quite evident on her olive skin. A purple bruise lined her jaw, while a brush burn left an angry red smudge down her right cheek and over to her dimpled chin. His gaze lowered to her right arm where her wrist was bandaged. Sofia had refused an X-ray, but the doctor was fairly certain her wrist was only sprained.

"Niko, did you hear me?"

He snapped out of his thoughts and stared into her eyes, trying to remember what she'd originally asked. Oh, yes, she wanted to know about the smile he'd been wearing. "Ah, it was nothing."

"It was definitely something if it actually had you smiling. Please tell me."

Had she just implied he didn't smile much? He'd never thought of that until now. Being around her had him considering things he'd never paused to think of before. What would it hurt to tell her the truth? "I was just remembering some childhood memories."

"Happy ones, I take it."

"Some were." *Happy* was a description he wouldn't readily attach to his past. Not wanting to go further down this path with her, he decided to change the subject. "You should be sitting down." He rushed to the couch and gathered the manila folders he'd been sorting. "Here you go."

Without an argument, she sat down. "I can't even imagine what it must have been like traveling the world as a kid. I spent most of my childhood in New York. We didn't vacation much. With so many kids, it got a bit costly." She stopped and pressed her lips together as though she'd said more than she'd intended.

"I guess traveling with my grandfather had its perks."

"You don't sound convinced."

He shrugged. "Sometimes I envied my roommate at school. He lived in a small village outside of London. He'd tell me about all of the things he did with his older brothers and his best friend." He shrugged. "You know kids—they always want something they don't have." It's what his grandfather always told him when he complained about not having any siblings or not being able to go to the mainland to play football.

"I'm so sorry."

"For what?" Niko wasn't accustomed to people feeling sorry for him.

"It sounds to me like you were a lonely little boy."

"I dealt with it."

"You mean you got used to it."

Was there a difference? Apparently Sofia thought so. He gave himself a mental shake. There was no point going down memory lane. He was no longer that bored kid. He was now a powerful businessman.

It was time to divert the conversation away from himself. "And how are you feeling now?"

"Better. That nap was exactly what I needed. But right now, if you aren't too busy, I'd really like to hear more about your childhood."

He sighed. "There's not much to tell."

"There's a lot to tell. I'd like to know more about the father of my child."

He shrugged. "You know everything that's important."

"Do I?" She arched a fine brow, challenging him.

Not about to be bullied into continuing to open up about his past, he pretended as though he hadn't heard Sofia's question. "Can I get you a pillow or a blanket? Should you even be out here?"

"The doctor said for me to rest. She didn't say I couldn't change rooms once in a while." She frowned. "Unless you're politely telling me to get lost."

"I'm not." And she did have a point. He knew she couldn't just lie around and do nothing. But it was for the sake of their child. "At least put your feet up and get comfortable." He followed her gaze to the coffee table littered with papers, files, books and a coffee mug. "I'll move them. Give me a second."

Just then the doorbell rang. When Sofia sent him a questioning glance, he said, "I'm expecting a delivery."

She nodded in understanding before he moved to the door. As anticipated, there was a courier waiting with a box from Niko's office in Greece. He quickly signed for it, accepted the weighty package and closed the door.

When he once again met Sofia's inquisitive gaze, he knew she was expecting the box to contain something exciting. "Sorry. It's just some files from the office."

"Do they have something to do with these?" Sofia pointed to the papers surrounding her on the couch.

"My grandfather was from a different generation and relied heavily on paper copy. It's going to take me quite a long time until I have everything in the computer system, but I'll do whatever is necessary to digitize everything."

He carried the large box over to the desk. Then he returned to Sofia to help gather the mess of reference material. When he set the papers down next to the box, they slid to the side, spilling all over the top of the desk. With a sigh, he accepted that he would deal with them later. Right now, he needed to tend to Sofia. He could only wonder what that might entail.

When he turned around, she was staring at him with a strange look on her face. "What?"

"That's a lot of paperwork. You must be working on a really important project."

He raked his fingers through his hair. "It's the biggest one of my career. But it doesn't matter now." What was he saying? It was all he'd thought about for the past couple of years. "The only thing that matters now is making sure you have everything you need."

"I'm fine. You don't have to worry about me."

She didn't look comfortable. Niko moved next to her and pushed aside the books and candles adorning the coffee table. Then he gently lifted her legs.

"Niko, what are you doing?"

"Making you comfy. You're supposed to keep your feet up." He carefully placed her legs on the glass tabletop. "Would you like to have a pillow under your feet?"

"You're being ridiculous. I'm fine. And I don't

remember the doctor saying anything specifically about keeping my feet up." She started to move when Niko sent her a stern look. "Fine. You win. But I don't need a pillow."

"What else can I get you? Something to drink?" Without bothering to wait for her answer, he moved to the fresh pitcher of water that he'd gotten for himself. He dropped cubes of ice into a tall glass and filled it up. "Here you go." He held the glass out to her. "I read that pregnant women should have plenty of water."

"You were reading up on pregnancy?" There was a very definite note of surprise in her voice.

Niko took a seat on one of the plush white armchairs a comfortable distance from her. Because every time they touched, an electric charge raced up his arm and short-circuited his thoughts. "How about some food? Or the television remote?"

"Did you really read up on babies and pregnancy?" Her direct gaze met his.

"I did." Why did that admission make him feel so uncomfortable? It wasn't as if he'd done anything wrong. Wasn't that what expectant fathers were supposed to do?

"I'm impressed."

"Impressed? With what?"

"With you. Somehow you've managed to care for me and still keep up with your business. You work really hard, and I'm guessing you don't have to."

He'd never considered not working. It was never an option, and, even if it had been, he wouldn't have taken it. He loved his position running the Stravos Trust. "I like to stay busy. If I'm not working, I'm reading."

He caught sight of her smile. In that moment, a spot warmed in his chest and radiated outward. He couldn't tell if it was from her compliment or the smile that lit up her face and made her eyes sparkle. He did his best not to dwell on why either should affect him so much.

"Really?" She tilted her head slightly to the side. "I guess I can see that. What do you like to read?"

Was she really interested in his reading habits? He knew for a fact that no woman had ever asked him about his reading preferences. Other women had been more interested in what famous people he knew or if he had connections to Hollywood or the fashion houses in Paris or Milan. Sofia was so different from all of them that he didn't know exactly what to make of her.

"I like to read nonfiction."

She nodded as though computing his answer. "So you like biographies and that sort of thing?"

"I do. And recounts of historic events. I also read a lot of periodicals."

"But what about fiction?"

He shook his head. "I don't bother with it."

"But why? There are some really great fiction books out there."

"I'd rather stick with reality."

"There's something to be said for using your imagination. It lets you see beyond the here and now and imagine something bigger and better."

Was she talking about her life? Was she unhappy with it? The more he knew about her, the more he wanted to know. "And what sorts of fiction books do you read?"

"Cozy mysteries and..."

"And?"

"Romance."

He couldn't help but smile. He should have known. She always struck him as the puppies, posies and rainbow type. Always looking for the good, even when it came to him—the man who'd gotten her pregnant. "So you believe in happily-ever-after?"

"You say that like it's some sort of crime."

"No. Not a crime. It's just that—"

He caught himself in time. He didn't want to ruin this friendly moment between them. It was a beginning, something he hoped they could build on. But not like the relationships in her books. He wouldn't sweep her off her feet and make a bunch of empty promises. But that didn't mean they couldn't be happy together—as friends—married friends.

"Just what?" Sofia sent him an expectant look.

He sighed. Why had he said anything at all? And then he realized it was easy to talk to Sofia. Too easy. "If you're looking to me for something romantic, you might as well know now that I'm not that kind of man."

"And why would that be an issue?" Her gaze narrowed. "I never once asked anything from you. I even told you to continue on your trip without me."

"And leave you here on your own?" He shook his head. "I don't think so. You need someone to make sure you listen to the doctor."

"And you've elected yourself to the task."

"I'm the only one around. And you're forgetting that I have a vested interest." A ding from his laptop alerted him of an upcoming Skype meeting. He got to his feet and moved toward the desk.

"You mean the baby?"

"Of course." What else did she think? He shut off the reminder. When he turned back to Sofia to tell her that he had a meeting in ten minutes, he was struck by her distinct frown. He inwardly groaned. He'd obviously said something wrong, but he wasn't quite sure what it might be.

"Oh." Her head lowered, shielding her expressive eyes from him.

And then it hit him. She wanted him to want to stay here for her. He wanted to tell her that he had, but the words wouldn't form.

He just couldn't get her hopes up that they'd walk off into the sunset hand in hand. Everyone he'd ever cared for had left him. He was better off remaining detached.

He'd been so young when his parents died that he couldn't remember much about them. And then his grandmother had died soon after. That left him with his grandfather, who Niko supposed loved him in his own way, but it wasn't the way a child needed to be loved. A string of nannies were not a suitable replacement. His child deserved better than that.

Niko wasn't going anywhere. And neither was Sofia.

For better or worse, they were in this together.

CHAPTER ELEVEN

WAS IT POSSIBLE to be bored in paradise?

Sofia sighed and thought of all the amazing places she could be exploring at this very moment, if only she'd been more careful. She gently patted her abdomen.

"A little boredom is worth it as long as you're safe, little one."

"Did you say something?" Niko appeared at the doorway of the bedroom.

She hadn't seen him since earlier that day when he'd made it abundantly clear that his only reason for being here was to ensure the health of their baby. She told herself that his response was exactly what she'd wanted him to say.

"I…I was just talking to the baby."

His eyes widened. "Do you really think it can hear you?"

"Maybe. Although at this stage, he's still pretty little."

"He? You think it's going to be a boy?"

She shrugged. "I don't know. But it's better than referring to the baby as an it."

Niko nodded in understanding. "I'm sorry to have been on that conference call for so long. You didn't have to stay in here the whole time. You must be hungry. What can I get you?"

"I need something, but it isn't food." When she noticed that she had his full attention, she said, "I need something to do." And she had an idea, but she wasn't so sure Niko would be agreeable.

He stepped farther into the room. "But you can't do anything. That's the point of bed rest."

"I'm bored." She groaned. "I at least need something to occupy my mind."

Niko rubbed his stubbled chin. "There are some more magazines in the other room. I'll get them for you."

"No, thanks. I've read most of them. And if I text Kyra one more time today, I'm pretty certain she'll block my number."

"I'm sure she understands."

She studied Niko. He hadn't shaved, and his hair was tousled. His usual "pressed suit" appearance had taken on a very casual look, which included a partially unbuttoned dress shirt with its fair share of wrinkles, dark slacks and bare feet. The man really needed some casual clothes, especially for times like this.

Not good at beating around the bush, she said, "Maybe I could help you."

"Me?" His eyes opened wide as though the suggestion came as a complete surprise. He shook his head. "I don't think so. You just rest. I have everything under control."

He turned for the door. He wasn't going to get away that easily. She slid her feet to the floor and stood. There had to be something she could do. She rushed after him.

"Niko." She called out his name from the edge of the living room.

He turned with a start. "What are you doing out of bed?"

"I'm serious about this. You obviously need help, and I need something to keep me busy."

He raked his fingers though his wavy dark hair. "What am I going to do with you? You're supposed to be relaxing." When she didn't say anything, he gestured to the couch. "Don't just stand there. Come sit down."

He moved his laptop to the side so she could have a seat. "Can I get you anything to eat or drink?"

"Some orange juice would be good. Thank you."

The suite had an open-floor concept, so it was easy for her to communicate with him while he got their refreshments. She couldn't take her eyes off him as he moved about the kitchen. He was so handsome even in his unshaven, shabby state. And there was something exceedingly sexy about a man waiting on her hand and foot.

But she felt guilty, too. She knew what a burden he'd inherited from his grandfather. The Stravos Trust appeared to be more like a life sentence than a blessing. Niko glanced over at her as he put together some finger foods with the juice. He smiled, but it didn't quite reach his eyes. She hated the thought that she was responsible for his exhaustion.

She turned to the papers on the couch. She started to gather them into an orderly pile to place on the coffee table, making room for Niko on the couch next to her. While she was straightening the papers, she noticed they were rows and rows of numbers. What in the world did he need with all of them?

"Here you go." Niko set a tray in front of her. "I thought you might be hungry."

She glanced down at the array of fruit, vegetables, crackers and dip. Now that she thought about it, she was a bit hungry. She reached for one of the plump strawberries. "Thank you."

"No problem. Here. Let me take those for you." He gestured toward the papers.

She relinquished the reports to him. "What are all of those papers?"

He waved off her question. "Nothing for you to worry about."

"But obviously you're worried about them." His handsome face was creased with worry lines, and his eyes were bloodshot from a lack of sleep. "I'd like to know, if you'll tell me."

He shrugged and then took a seat next to her. "If you really want to know, it's my support to justify changing the way the Stravos Trust does business. My grandfather was a big believer in spreading out our assets to keep them safe. Not too much in one place so that if a sector went under, it didn't affect us much."

She nodded. "That makes sense. It's a very conservative way of doing business. But I take it you don't agree."

"I don't. I think the older my grandfather got, the more cautious he got. To the point where I believe he spread our assets too thinly. Without some risk, there can't be any real growth."

Sofia enjoyed their conversation. She loved listening as Niko explained his plan to sell off certain assets and focus more on the shipping sector by purchasing one of the world's largest containerships. She loved the passion that filled his voice when he spoke about the future he envisioned for his company.

"And these numbers, what are they for?" She gestured toward the papers and files that had been moved to the chair.

"They are the backup I need to consolidate and send to my advisers."

She found that interesting. "So you won't just forge ahead on your own?"

He shook his head. "There's too much at stake. That's why I have a panel of experts. They will analyze the data and advise me of their take on matters."

"But why are you personally compiling all of this data?" It was only after she'd uttered the words that she realized the answer. She was the reason he was here in a luxurious suite, slaving away instead of in his fully staffed office in

Greece. Guilt weighed on her like a waterlogged coat—heavy and uncomfortable.

"It's best this way. I need to make sure everything is done correctly. If the numbers are skewed, even slightly, it could sway decisions one way or the other."

This was her chance to pay him back in a small way for caring for her since her accident. "Let me help."

His brows drew together. "Are you serious?"

"Of course I am. Why wouldn't I be?"

He shook his head. "You don't need to bother with this. Your job is to rest and take care of that baby. That's more important."

"And so is my sanity. I need something to do that will distract me."

"I'll go downstairs to the lobby and get you some more magazines. I'll also see if I can find you some books to read."

She realized he wasn't trying to be nice and watching out for the baby. He was rejecting her offer because he didn't think she was up to the task. He thought that a maid had no business helping him with something so important. And maybe he was right. Maybe it was beyond her current capabilities, but she was a fast learner. Instead of even considering her offer, he'd outright dismissed it. The rejection stung.

She averted her gaze, not about to let him read her thoughts as he'd done so many times in the past. Because there was no way she could hide the hurt at knowing he didn't think she was up to the task of assisting him.

Darn it. Now, the backs of her eyes stung. She would not cry. She flat out refused. Blast, these pregnancy hormones were making her so emotional. She blinked repeatedly, willing her emotions under control.

She pushed aside the rest of the fruit, vegetables and crackers. She'd lost her appetite. "You're right. I don't know what I was thinking. I think I'll go lay down for a bit."

She ignored the surprised look on his face and headed for the bedroom. When she got there, she sent the door flying shut with a resounding thud. It didn't make her feel any better like she'd been hoping it would.

All she wanted was to be alone with her wounded ego. If Niko thought so little of her skills, how was she ever going to get a college administrator to take her seriously? And without furthering her education, how would she do right by their child?

She'd just flopped down on the bed when there was a tap at the door. She wasn't ready to play nice—not yet. "Go away."

"Sofia, let me in. I didn't mean to upset you." A few minutes passed before he added, "Please, Sofia. Hear me out."

She had the distinct impression he wasn't going anywhere until she heard him out. She swiped at her damp cheeks and blew her nose. "Fine. Come in."

Was it possible he had a sheepish look on his face? The great and powerful Nikolas Stravos III looked as though he'd done something wrong. The ache in her chest eased a bit.

He cleared his throat. "Listen, about what I said. I only said it because...well, I don't want you doing my work because you feel sorry for me."

He thought she'd made the offer out of sympathy? *Really?* She searched his eyes, finding sincerity in them. He hadn't rejected her offer because he doubted her capability. It had nothing to do with her and everything to do with him. She struggled not to grin. Really, these pregnancy hormones lent themselves to big mood swings. It wasn't as though he'd said he loved her. Not that she wanted him to say anything like that.

"I don't feel sorry for you." She hoped that was the right response. "I truly wanted to help. I'm interested in learning more about what you do."

He didn't say a word for a moment as though considering his options. "There is one other problem. We only have one laptop, and we both can't work on it at once."

"Oh." That was a problem. And one she didn't have an easy solution for.

He glanced at her. "Were you serious when you said you wanted to lie down?"

She shrugged. Would it make her look pathetic if she were to admit she was sleepy? She hadn't slept well the night before as she kept having some bizarre nightmares.

"Tell you what. If you promise to stay in bed and take a nap or watch a movie, I'll run out and pick up another laptop."

"For me?" This time a smile pulled at her lips, and she didn't fight it. She loved the idea of working side by side with him. And she could use the access to the internet to move ahead with her college applications.

"Yes, for you. Do you promise not to move? I don't want to have to worry about you."

"I promise." When he started for the door, she

called out, "Wait. Can you pick me up one more thing?"

His brow arched. "It depends on what you have in mind."

"Ice cream."

He smiled. "I think that's doable. What flavor?"

"Cookie dough. No. Um, rocky road. But cherry vanilla is good, too."

Niko laughed again. "I guess the cravings are kicking in. How about I get an assortment?"

She gave him a big smile. "Thank you. Not only for the ice cream, but also for trusting me with your work. I won't let you down."

"I never thought you would."

Her heart swelled. She would prove herself to him. She would do whatever he wanted, and she'd do a good job. After all, she'd excelled at math in school. She couldn't wait to get started.

CHAPTER TWELVE

THIS WAS GOING better than she'd imagined.

Sofia stared out the floor-to-ceiling windows at the Pacific Ocean. It'd been a week since her accident, and to her utter surprise Niko had stayed with her the entire time. He waited on her hand and foot.

The only movement she was allowed was bathroom breaks and to move her fingers over the keyboard. And even with that, he made her take breaks, which included naps. She hadn't realized how run-down she'd been feeling. Her aches and pains from the fall had eased, though some ugly green-and-yellow bruises still remained.

But Niko kept her distracted. All week he'd patiently explained her tasks in terms she could understand. He surprised her with his patience in showing her how to read the reports and how to input the data into the computer. He was teaching her to use a spreadsheet program, and that was a skill she could use to make herself more attractive to college administrators and future employers.

The only drawback to this new arrangement was that it got a bit lonely. Even with them cooped up in this luxurious suite, Niko made sure they didn't spend too much time together. When she was in the bedroom, he was in the living room. When she was in the living room, he was in the bedroom. If she ever needed a sign that he wasn't interested in her, this was it.

"Are you ready for lunch?" Niko strolled into the living room as though her thoughts had summoned him.

She glanced up, catching sight of his week-old beard. It was filling in nicely, but she preferred him clean shaven. "You know you don't have to fuss over me anymore. Didn't you hear the doctor this morning? I'm fine to return to my normal activities."

He nodded. "I heard her. But she also said not to overdo it."

"And I don't think preparing lunch is overdoing it. And then I plan to start cleaning the suite." When he didn't say anything, her curiosity got the better of her. "Aren't you going to say anything?"

"Why should I? You have that look on your face."

"What look?" She had a look? What did it say? She didn't like the thought that Niko was getting to know her well enough to read her expressions.

"The look that says you're about to do what you want no matter what I say."

"Is that what you really think? I've been the perfect patient."

"Hmph." Niko crossed his arms over his muscular chest. "Where shall I start? The laundry you insisted on doing when I stepped out to pick up a few items at the store? Or the beds that you had to make up—"

"It's my job."

"Right now, your job is taking care of that little one—"

"I am," she said defensively, still feeling guilty for the fall. That would never happen again."

"I know, and I just want to make things easier for you. I don't want anything to happen to you. Seeing you fall, well, I never felt so helpless. I've never been so scared."

Was it possible he cared about her maybe just a little? Before her imagination got carried away, she halted it. He meant he was scared about the baby's health. That had to be it.

"Don't worry. I won't overdo it. I promise. Now, I should make those salads." She moved toward the kitchen. "After lunch, I'll get started cleaning the suite. If you want to go through the rooms and mark everything that needs to be packaged and shipped back to Greece, that would be helpful."

Niko's phone buzzed. He checked the screen before returning the phone to his pocket. He frowned but didn't say anything. What was bothering him? The message on his phone? Or had she forgotten to do something?

She pressed her hands to her hips. "What's wrong?"

"Nothing." He glanced away. "I'm hungry is all."

She didn't believe him. "Is it something I said?"

"I swear it isn't you." When she continued to stare at him, prompting him with her eyes for a better answer, he added, "Fine. If you must know, I've been experiencing a lot of resistance to my proposal."

She breathed easier knowing he wasn't upset with her. "You mean the one I helped you complete?"

He nodded. "All but one of my advisers have outright rejected it."

"But why? The numbers are sound. We made sure of it."

"It's not that. They are opposed to my dramatic restructuring."

She was trying to follow him, but she was missing something. "I'm not understanding the problem."

"These are men my grandfather employed for many years. They are used to doing things in a certain way—my grandfather's way."

"And they are resisting what you are trying to do with the company?" When Niko nodded, she asked, "Can you hire your own people?"

"I've thought about it, but these people are experts at what they do. I don't want to let them go. They accepted the changes to the human resources policies, but they had issues with some internal restructuring I initiated. And now with the proposal to sell off some subsidiaries in order to invest heavily in the shipping sector, they don't even want to consider it—"

"Whoa. Slow down. That sounds like a lot."

"They are changes my grandfather should have implemented years ago."

"Did you ever consider you might be moving too fast? What if you slow down and give your employees time to catch on to your plan? Then they could be your strongest allies."

His brows scrunched together. "But I can't just stop."

"I'm not suggesting you stop everything, but maybe pick the most important change and focus on it for a while before moving on to the next item on your list."

"I don't know."

"It stands to reason that people naturally resist change. But time usually gives people a different perspective."

"And that would work for you? Giving you time to adjust to a new situation or a new way of doing things?"

"There's no promise, but it certainly wouldn't hurt." She smiled, liking that he was asking for her input.

Her ex had never asked her opinion about anything important. Bobby thought that business and money were a man's domain and cooking and laundry were a woman's. She'd talked herself into believing with time she'd be able to change Bobby's opinion. That had never happened. It was foolish of her to believe her love could change someone.

"Thanks for giving me something to consider." Niko's voice drew her out of her thoughts. "Now, how about I repay you by taking you out to eat?"

"I don't think it's a good idea."

Niko paused as though considering her words. "You mean because of the baby? Are you having pains again? You didn't say anything at the doctor's—"

"No, it's not that. The baby is fine."

"Honest?"

She nodded. She would never lie about something so important. "It's just that we've been in Hawaii much longer than anticipated. If I don't get started cleaning, we won't be able to take off tomorrow evening."

He waved away her worries. "The cleaning can wait. This is more important."

"You're serious?"

"I'm always serious when it comes to food." He ran a hand over his flat abs. "You've got to be hungry, too. Let's go try some local cuisine."

The eager look on his face said that fighting him would be fruitless. In all honesty, she'd been so nervous that morning before her doctor's appointment that she'd barely eaten a thing. She glanced down at her T-shirt and casual shorts. "Is the restaurant going to be fancy?"

"It doesn't have to be. There's a place along the beach that I've heard people raving about. So do we have a lunch date?"

Her lips pursed together as she tried to conceal her surprise at him using the word *date* where she was concerned. She was certain he hadn't intended any romantic connotation. So then why did she have this funny feeling in her chest?

He eyed her as though waiting for her response. She really did want to get out of the hotel. As beautiful and luxurious as it was, she'd been in the same suite for a week. She was going a little stir-crazy. "But what about your proposal?"

"I think I'll take your advice and let my advisers think about it for a bit before I speak with them again. And I'm sure my other staff will appreciate a break in the long string of emails I've been sending them."

She pulled her shoulders back. "Sounds like a good plan."

"Let me just get cleaned up. I won't be long." He started toward the guest room as he'd insisted she take the spacious master suite. Then he turned back. "Well, don't just stand there. Sit down and rest. I don't want you overdoing it today."

"Did anyone ever tell you that you're bossy?"

"Yes. But that isn't going to get me to change my mind. We don't want any return visits to the doctor, at least not any unexpected visits."

She shook her head. "The next thing you know you'll be wrapping me in cotton for the next six months."

"You know, now that you mentioned it—"

"Don't you dare!" She moved to the couch, grabbed one of the plush throw pillows and tossed it at him.

He caught it with ease and tossed it back to her. The deep rumble of his laughter filled the air as he moved back into the hallway. It was the first time she'd heard him laugh since that one magical night at the wedding. Why did it feel as if it were now a lifetime ago?

As close as she and Niko had become during this trip, she'd never felt so distant from someone. Except when it came to work, then Niko was 100 percent present and attentive. But when the work was done for the day, it was as though he put up a wall between them. No wonder he didn't want a family. He didn't have time for one—or he was purposely making excuses to avoid having one.

But during their banter, she'd noticed a subtle shift in their relationship. Was it possible that the protective wall around his heart had started to crumble? Maybe not completely. But even a crack or two was progress, wasn't it?

But to what end? Was he interested in developing some sort of relationship with her? Or was he just interested in her because she was the mother of his baby?

CHAPTER THIRTEEN

HE WAS A MESS.

Niko stared at his image in the mirror. *Wow!* His hair was unruly and his beard—well, he had one now. He'd never been anything but clean shaven in his life. And his eyes were bloodshot. No wonder Sofia had been giving him strange looks off and on this week.

He had been pushing himself hard—real hard. He'd been so eager to prove himself to everyone—most of all himself—that he could step into his grandfather's shoes at the helm of the Stravos Trust. In the process, he hadn't noticed the unhappiness he'd been inflicting on everyone—including himself.

He scratched at his beard. Between watching over Sofia and keeping up with the office via videoconferencing and emails, he hadn't had two minutes to call his own this past week. He reached for his razor. This mess was going to take a bit of time to tame, but he wanted to look good for Sofia.

He'd noticed how she'd perked up when he mentioned getting her out of the hotel. He couldn't blame her. They were visiting a tropical paradise, but instead of sightseeing and lounging about on the beach, they'd been huddled away in this suite working.

Sofia deserved to get out and enjoy some of Hawaii. And now that he'd finally completed his long-range business plan and had submitted it to his advisory board, he could afford to take a break.

Oh, who was he kidding? The thing bothering him was how Sofia pushed to get a move on their trip. Was she that anxious for their time together to be over? Once they reached New York, her home, he had a feeling he'd lose any chance to win her over. His hands moved faster, trying to eradicate himself of the bushy growth covering his jaw and upper lip.

He'd enjoyed this past week. Not the part where he'd been worried about Sofia and the baby, but the part of being there for her. No one had ever needed him before. His grandfather had been a solitary man who prided himself on his independence. Having someone rely on him in a personal way was new to Niko, and he liked it—he liked Sofia. She was very strong and determined, more so than he'd ever imagined. He respected that about her.

Time was ticking. And this time he wasn't contemplating a business deal. This time it was something so much more important. Sooner rather than later he needed to propose his idea of them getting married. But how would she react?

He rushed through the shower and soon appeared in the living room to find that Sofia had changed into a summer dress. It had a white bodice with some blue flowers on it and a dark blue skirt. It was loose fitting, obscuring her figure. He liked the way she looked. She was perfect, with curves in all the right places.

"Is there something wrong with what I'm wearing?" She smoothed a hand down over the skirt as though straightening a nonexistent wrinkle.

"Um, no. Not at all. It looks nice on you. Is it new?"

She shook her head, but her gaze didn't quite meet his. There was something amiss, but for the life of him, he couldn't figure out what was the matter. He wasn't good at circling problems. In business, he trudged forth and dealt pointedly with the issue. It was the most efficient way to resolve matters.

When she didn't answer him, he said, "Sofia, look at me."

When she lifted her head, her eyes glistened with unshed tears. *What in the world?* His chest tightened. Tears made him feel so out of control, so unsure of himself. *Please don't let it be the baby.* "Are you feeling all right? If not, we can stay in?"

She blinked repeatedly and shook her head. "You're hungry. We should go."

"Not until you tell me what's the matter."

She shrugged. "You'll think it's foolish."

"Let me be the judge."

Her gaze moved to the white-tiled floor. "My clothes don't fit. I sat around this week doing nothing but eating, and now nothing fits. I had to wear this because it's one of the few things I could squeeze into. I'm fat."

That was it? That was what had her so upset? He let out a breath. "You are not getting fat." He stepped closer to her and placed a finger beneath her chin so their eyes met. "You are pregnant.

Our baby is growing within you. Be happy. If it's clothes you need, we'll get you some."

"But I don't have the extra money—"

"Hush. Remember, you work for me. Between polishing up the suite in Tokyo and helping me complete the proposal, you've earned yourself a whole new wardrobe."

She sent him a hesitant look. "I don't want your charity."

"Trust me—it's not charity. You truly earned it."

"You really think so?"

"I do." She'd really impressed him. "Now let's go. We have a busy afternoon." He started for the door and opened it for her.

"I did do all of that, didn't I? I think I have earned a bonus." She sent him a playful smile.

"You do, huh?"

"Most definitely. After all, good help is so hard to find."

He chuckled, broadening her smile. "I'll give it due consideration."

"I knew you'd see things my way." As she went to pass him, she paused. "You know, I could pick out some new clothes for you while we're at it." She ran a finger down the lapel of his suit jacket. "Something more casual."

There was a determined tone to her voice that set off an alarm in his mind. He had a feeling if he wasn't careful, she'd be updating more than just his wardrobe and at a faster pace than he was attempting to implement his plans at the Stravos Trust.

Now he understood what Sofia had meant when she said his employees would resist change. He liked his pressed dress shirts and suits. He felt in control in them. He didn't need casual clothes. He was fine just the way he was.

But when she gazed back at him, he found himself getting lost in her big brown eyes. Was it possible he'd already lost the battle and they hadn't even stepped in a store yet?

The next morning Sofia put on one of her new maternity outfits. She never thought stretchy material would ever have a place in her wardrobe. She'd always made a point of making sure her clothes fit perfectly, but that was no longer the case.

She ran a hand over her slightly rounded abdomen. "You're changing everything, aren't you?"

"I assume you're not talking to me."

She jumped at the sound of Niko's voice. She turned on her heels. "I didn't hear you come in."

"Sorry. I didn't mean to interrupt your conversation with the baby. You do that a lot. Is it important to the baby's development?"

"How much do you know about babies?"

He sighed. "Honestly, absolutely nothing."

"Then, Mr. Stravos, it's my turn to teach you a thing or two." She enjoyed the fact she knew more about this subject than he did. Somehow it made her feel as though they were at last on even ground.

"You're going to teach me? How do you know so much?"

"Did I mention the really big family I have in New York? None of my brothers have settled down yet, but I have a couple dozen cousins, most of whom have kids now. So there's always baby stuff going on. You don't have any extended family?"

He shook his head. "My only cousin is Kyra, and, as you know, we didn't meet until recently."

"I know. Let's stop by the bookstore. But we'll have to hurry. What time is our flight?"

"The flight?"

She frowned at him. "Is there a problem?"

Niko rubbed the back of his neck like she'd seen him do numerous times when his business plans hit a snag and he was devising a way to fix the problem. "About that. I didn't remember to contact the pilot—"

"What? But how?" She wanted to be angry with him, honestly she did, but she just couldn't muster the emotion.

"I guess I got distracted with all of the clothes shopping." He stepped back as though to admire her new outfit. "And we did a mighty fine job. You look beautiful."

She put her hands on her hips. "If we did so great, why are you wearing another suit? Why aren't you wearing any of the casual clothes we picked out?"

His gaze avoided hers. "I, ah, didn't think of it."

"You do know I don't believe you, right?"

"Tell you what. I'll change into some of those new clothes you picked out for me if I get to pick out what we do this afternoon."

"I'll be cleaning—"

"I don't think so. I have plans for you."

Well, that was certainly cryptic enough. And then she caught a gleam in his eyes. What exactly was he up to? And just how much should she trust him?

"Oh, come on," he cajoled her. "Surely I'm not

that untrustworthy." And then he smiled, sending her heart tumbling.

Now why did he have to go and do that. His smile was like a warm sunbeam, and it dissolved her resistance to his charms like a hot knife through butter. Oh, she was so pathetic where he was concerned.

It was just a small delay. Not a big deal. "Okay. You have a deal. Go change."

She had no idea what she'd set herself up for, but something told her it'd be worth it. Just the thought of spending the day with Niko had her grinning and her heart beating faster. What adventure did he have in store for them?

CHAPTER FOURTEEN

Now, THIS WAS the way to spend a sunny afternoon.

The wind combed through Niko's hair, scattering it. And he didn't care as he sat next to Sofia on the sailboat he'd chartered for the afternoon. It'd come with its own crew, so instead of Niko manning the helm as he did back in Greece, he had time to spend with Sofia.

And his plan appeared to be a success. She was smiling as her eyes glittered with happiness. And the sun was putting some color in her pale cheeks. This was exactly what she needed. A distraction far from computers, cleaning supplies and baby books.

"Are you enjoying yourself?" He glanced over at her.

"I am. You know, this is my first time sailing."

"And it won't be your last." When her eyes widened, he realized he'd vocalized his thoughts. Still, it was a chance to find out if she was warming up to the possibility of them marrying—for their child's sake. "I have a boat back in Greece. You're welcome to use it anytime."

He didn't know until that point how much he wanted her to take him up on the offer. He'd thought he was fine continuing to live a solitary existence, but he'd come to find out how much he enjoyed spending time with Sofia, whether they were cleaning a suite, sharing a meal or boating. Some things were just better when they were shared with another.

Sofia pressed a hand to his shoulder, drawing him from his meandering thoughts. "It sounds like a lovely idea, but I don't think I'll be getting back to Greece anytime soon—not with the baby on the way, my job and going back to school."

"I understand. But know that the invitation is always open." He took it as a good sign that she hadn't outright turned him down.

Perhaps she'd be more receptive to his idea after their outing. He'd learned during his apprenticeship at the Stravos Trust not to hesitate when a prime opportunity presented itself. However, his gut was telling him this wasn't the time to propose. But it would be soon.

Sofia gazed out over the tranquil waters. "Growing up so close to the sea, you must have done this all of the time."

"Done what? You mean sailing?" When she nodded, he said, "I'm afraid not."

"Really? I assumed you and your grandfather would go boating almost every day."

"My grandfather had one love, and that was his work. He didn't have time for sailing or fishing or anything else that didn't pertain to an earnings or loss report."

"What about your parents? I know you mentioned your father passed away, but before that, did you two go boating or fishing together? Or maybe you did with your mother?"

He glanced at her. She really didn't know about his past? It wasn't any secret. Anyone with a computer could type in his name and pull up his family history. The look in Sofia's eyes said she was genuinely curious. What would it hurt to tell her a bit? After all, she was carrying the next Stravos.

"My parents died in a car accident when I was five. So I don't remember a whole lot about them."

"Oh, I didn't know. I'm so sorry."

All of this talk was too depressing and not what he'd intended for today. "I'm sure you don't want to hear about this."

Sofia reached out to him, placing her hand on his thigh. "I do, if you're willing to share. I figure if we're going to coparent, we should know more about each other."

"What about you?" he asked, turning the conversation away from himself.

"Okay, I'll go first. What would you like to know?"

He stifled a sigh, knowing already that she came from a normal family—something he'd never had. "Are your parents still alive?"

"Alive and still happily married after almost forty years. In fact, it's disgusting how much they are still in love. Talk about lots of PDA. Sometimes it's like they're still teenagers." Her face scrunched up into a grossed-out expression as she shook her head, making him laugh.

"They sound very happy." He couldn't imagine what it must be like to grow up in such a loving home. Her parents proved there were exceptions to every rule. He was glad for Sofia's sake that her parents were the exception. But love was still such a risk with very high stakes. "How about your brothers? Are you close with them?"

She shrugged. "I'm the little sister with four overprotective brothers."

"So you have a big family." He'd always wanted to be a part of a large family, but that was not to be. It was a possibility for their child. His heart *thump-thumped* at the idea of coming home from the office to Sofia and a houseful of kids. "Would you like to have more kids?"

"I…I don't know." She got a sad look on her face. "I thought so at one point, but everything has changed dramatically since then."

He knew she was thinking about the baby she'd lost. He had absolutely no idea what that must be like, and his heart went out to her. He reached out and squeezed her hand. "This time around will be different."

"I know." She expelled a sorrowful sigh. "But I've changed, too. I don't want the same things that I did at one time."

His gut tightened. "Are you talking about marriage?"

She nodded. "The baby and I will be fine on our own."

"I hope there'll be room for me."

"Oh, of course. I didn't mean to imply you wouldn't have a place in the baby's life."

"Good. I don't want him…or her growing up like I did, never getting to know my parents."

Sofia tightened her fingers around his, reminding him that they were still linked. "That won't happen with our son or daughter. They'll know us and how much we love them."

"Do you think by knowing your big family that our child will feel cheated by not having any siblings?"

"I don't know. I've never really given it much thought. A large family can be chaotic. This way our child won't feel lost in the shuffle."

"Like you did?"

She nodded. "I was the youngest and always felt left out of things because I was too small."

"Surely it couldn't have been all bad."

"It wasn't. We had a lot of good times, too. Especially when the holidays rolled around."

"Would your brothers approve of me?" Niko didn't know why, but it mattered to him.

"I don't know."

Not exactly the stellar endorsement he'd been hoping for, but Sofia was probably being realistic. "I bet they'd kick my butt for knocking up their little sister."

"They'd probably try."

"Do they know yet? About the baby?"

"I didn't think that was news to share over the

phone. If I had, my brothers would have hunted you down already." Then she smiled, letting him know she teasing him.

He sighed. "You're lucky."

"Lucky? For having overprotective brothers?" She shook her head. "I don't think so. You have no idea how difficult it was to date with them lurking about. My mother at one point had to warn them off. If she hadn't, I'd have never had a date for the prom."

Niko didn't know what it was like to experience that sort of love, but he felt as though he'd missed out on something very special. The thought of his child growing up in such a loving family filled Niko with some comfort. He just had to make sure there was a permanent place in Sofia and their child's life for him.

Theirs wouldn't be a marriage of love. It would be better. From what he'd witnessed, most of the time love didn't last. Her parents were the exception. Even Sofia couldn't argue that point after her relationship with her ex had crumbled. Niko's body tensed as he thought of her coping with the loss of her first baby alone. He hoped for that man's sake that their paths never crossed.

No, his marriage to Sofia would be the best. It

would be built on friendship and mutual respect. Those were things that could withstand the test of time, unlike love, which was here one day and gone the next—

"Excuse me, Mr. Stravos."

The sound of the crewman's voice stirred Niko from his thoughts. "Yes?"

"Sir, we're here."

"Thank you. Just give us a minute or two."

The man nodded and strolled off.

"Where are we?" Sofia's face lit up with interest.

"I thought we'd go ashore for lunch."

She glanced over at the small island and then back at him. "Here?" Her shoulders grew rigid. "But...but it looks deserted. Surely you don't expect us to catch our own lunch and cook it over an open flame."

He couldn't help but laugh at the appalled look on her pretty face. "Relax. I had a picnic lunch packed for us, including a big blanket."

"Oh." Her shoulders eased, and the smile came back to her face. "So it's an adventure?"

"Yes, it is."

She glanced out at the blue water surrounding the boat. "But how will we get to shore?"

He struggled to maintain a serious expression. "You don't swim?"

"Niko, be serious. I don't have a swimsuit."

"There's nothing wrong with skinny-dipping."

"Niko!" Her cheeks filled with color.

Her outrage was his undoing. He broke down in laughter. When she crossed her arms and frowned at him, he gathered himself. "I take it the skinny-dipping idea doesn't appeal to you?"

"No." Her voice held a tone of finality. She glanced at the blue water again as the sun's rays danced on it and then turned back to him. "Why don't we just eat here? The boat is huge. We could even eat out here on the deck."

"I thought you had an adventurous spirit."

She frowned. "I left it at home with my swimsuit."

"Oh. Okay. Well, don't worry. You'll dry fast in the sun."

Her very kissable lips puckered together as she glared at him.

He couldn't remember the last time he'd had such an enjoyable day. Growing up, he'd only had one friend in his life to joke around with, Adam, his roommate at boarding school. That seemed like a lifetime ago. Niko had forgotten what it was like to let loose and enjoy himself.

"Relax." He didn't want her getting seriously upset with him and ruining the day. "There's a dinghy on board. We'll take that ashore."

She lowered her arms. "Were you enjoying having fun at my expense?"

"Perhaps." A broad smile pulled at his lips. "It's just so much fun. You get this little *V* between your brows, and your nose flares—"

"It does not." She fingered the tip of her nose.

"Don't worry. It's adorable."

"You are not funny, mister." She poked him in the chest. "I'm going to do with you what I do with my brothers and stop believing you."

"Is that so?"

She nodded.

"So if I told you I intended to extend our stay here in Hawaii, would you believe me?"

"No, I wouldn't. You're already so far behind on your schedule. In fact, we shouldn't even be here now. I should be cleaning the suite so we can leave."

"You'd rather be cleaning than enjoying this beautiful day?"

"I didn't say that."

"Good." He glanced around at the amazing view. He hadn't felt this free in years. "I couldn't think of anywhere I'd rather be."

"In the middle of the Pacific Ocean with no contact with civilization?"

"Don't forget about the amazing company." He loved making her smile.

"Are you always such a flirt?"

"Only on special occasions." He halted himself from saying more—from admitting that she was very special indeed. He didn't want to do anything to scare her off and ruin this moment. He got to his feet. "Now let me get our lunch. It's below deck."

He disappeared down the steps into the teak-wood interior of the ninety-foot sailboat. Everything gleamed. His friend who owned it certainly took excellent care of it.

"Can I get something for you, sir?" A deckhand appeared before him. The young man in a pressed white shirt and shorts appeared eager to please.

"I just came to get our picnic basket."

"Certainly, sir. I have it right here."

Niko had to admit this truly was an adventure. He'd never once delayed work to entertain a woman. He'd never even considered it. And yet here he was in khaki shorts, short sleeves and deck shoes, getting ready to have lunch with the most amazing woman on a small deserted island. And he couldn't be happier. How did that happen?

This was some adventure all right.

Wait until I tell Kyra about this. She'll never believe it.

Lunch on a deserted island with the world's hottest billionaire. This must be a dream. And I sure hope I don't wake up any time soon.

Sofia turned to Niko as he leaned back on his elbows, staring out at the horizon. His long legs were stretched out in front of him on the blanket. This was one of those rare times when he looked at ease.

They'd picked a private spot on the beach that was shaded by palm trees. A gentle breeze came in off the ocean and scattered his hair. She loved how he wore it a bit longer than most in his prominent position. The dark strands were finger-combed back off his handsome face. His gaze met hers, sending her heart racing. He was quite a package.

"Did you say something?"

Was it possible she'd vocalized her thoughts? Surely not. "Um, no."

He cast her a sideways glance as though not sure he believed her. Then he turned away. "You know, I was doing some thinking about the trip."

And here it came, his announcement that it was time they got back to business. She knew this cozy relationship couldn't go on forever. The sooner she got back to reality, the easier it would be for all concerned. She braced herself for his next words.

He cleared his throat. "And I was thinking we should stay here a bit longer."

"What?" This was not what she was expecting him to say. Not at all. "But why?"

He shrugged. "Why not?" Then he sat upright. "You're enjoying yourself, aren't you?"

"Well, yes, but we both know that…that it can't last."

He arched a dark brow. "Are you referring to the trip? Or to us?"

"I…um…" There was an us? She searched his eyes, looking for answers. But there was a wall up, keeping her out. She must be imagining things, only hearing what she wanted to hear. "I meant that we need to get a move on with closing up the suites. You have to get back to your office, and I have to get situated back in New York."

"The work can wait," he said nonchalantly.

"Are you serious?" What had happened to the real Niko—the man who was connected to his cell phone, who had the courier service on speed dial and conducted Skype meetings daily?

"Perhaps the problem is I'm trying to micromanage every part of the company, to show myself that I'm worthy of stepping into my grandfather's shoes and living up to my father's memory. It's a lot of pressure—pressure I'm putting on myself."

"And now?"

"Now I'm starting to realize I could sacrifice my whole life and happiness and still not measure up to my grandfather's standards. He was a force to be reckoned with in the business world."

"But you are, too."

Niko shrugged. "Perhaps. But I think I'm making everyone at the office miserable in the process."

"And what's your solution?"

"To lighten up. To let people do their jobs and show them that I trust them to do what they've been trained to do without second-guessing them constantly."

She knew this was a huge step for him. She'd watched him ever since they'd left Greece. He constantly reviewed and questioned things. He knew every part of his business. Could he really take a step back? She had a hard time believing it. Once a control freak, always a control freak.

"You don't believe me." The corner of his mouth lifted, and his eyes twinkled.

"What? I didn't say that."

"You didn't have to. It's written all over your face. You don't think I can let go."

Darn it. Why did her thoughts always have to filter over her face? She'd never had this problem with anyone before. It just seemed Niko could read her so well. "You do have to admit that it's easier said than done."

"Then let me prove it to you." He sat up straight. "For starters, I'm extending our stay in Hawaii."

"But why?"

His shoulders rose and fell. "I have stuff to do here."

"Stuff, huh? Could you be any more vague?"

"Was that a complaint?" He arched a brow. "Are you saying you don't want to stay here in paradise with me?"

She glanced around at the blue skies and tranquil water, but quite soon her gaze was drawn back to him. Her heart pounded faster. It didn't matter where they were, his presence would make it special. "And if I said yes, would you work the whole time, leaving me to explore the island by myself?"

"I told you—I'm going to change my ways."

She wanted to believe him, but she just couldn't imagine a man of his vast power and wealth kicking back and letting others make the big decisions. "I'm trying to believe you."

"What if I give you some proof?"

What would it hurt to have him put some action behind his words? "What do you have in mind?"

His hands moved over on the blanket. His fingers gently stroked hers, sending a tremor of excitement through her body. She searched his face for answers, but she didn't know the questions. Her mind was a frantic mess of fragmented thoughts.

His attention dipped to her lips. Her heart jumped into her throat, cutting off her breath. Was it wrong that she willed him to kiss her? It seemed like forever since their lips had touched.

Yet this was exactly what she'd promised herself she wouldn't do—fall for his charms. He would love her and leave her. She already had scars on her heart. She didn't need more.

The tip of her tongue moistened her dry lips.

But he was here, and this place was like some sort of dream. A tug-of-war waged within her—logic versus a deep yearning.

Niko captured her lips with his, taking the decision out of her hands. And for that she was grateful. Because once their lips touched, her thoughts fled. All she had to do now was enjoy. She would deal with the ramifications later—much later.

She leaned back on the blanket, pulling him down on top of her. She would never forget this day—this trip—this man. Ever.

CHAPTER FIFTEEN

AT LAST HE had the answer.

Niko had researched his options. Thought it through. And had come up with a strategic plan. Now he just needed the perfect time to put it all into action.

He smiled. It'd been a week of sightseeing, a couple of luaus, moonlit strolls along the beach and that amazing picnic on the deserted island where they'd made love. Niko couldn't remember being happier. He liked making Sofia smile.

As they climbed to the top of Diamond Head, he felt as if he were climbing to the top of the world. He glanced at Sofia. "Sure you don't need to rest?"

She paused and turned to him. "No. Let's keep going. Unless you need to rest."

Her face was a bit flushed. Oh, no, had they overdone it today? He'd tried to talk her out of the climb, but she'd insisted she felt perfectly fine, and the doctor had given her the all clear to return to her everyday routine. Niko suggested that climbing to the top of Diamond Head wasn't part of her everyday routine, but she'd brushed off his concerns.

"Do you want some more water?" He glanced down at the bottle in his hand, finding it more than half full.

"That's okay. I'm good."

"Why don't we sit down?" Niko suggested.

"Here?" Her forehead scrunched up. "We'd be in everyone's way sitting on the steps. Besides, we're almost there."

"Are you sure you feel all right?"

"What's the matter with you?"

With him? She was the one who looked pale. "Maybe we should turn back."

"And miss the view? No way." She continued ascending the mountain, one step after the other. "I'll beat you to the top," she called over her shoulder.

Her voice sounded chipper. Perhaps he was worried about nothing. He had to admit that her fall the other week had scared him more than he'd been willing to let on to her or even to himself until now. And he'd do anything to keep her and the baby safe.

He paused on the steps as a sense of protectiveness settled in. This was new to him. He'd never felt this way toward another human. It left him feeling a little off-kilter and a bit out of control because no matter what he did, he could never fully protect Sofia or the baby. But his plan would go a long way toward ensuring their safety. Which made him all the more certain his plan was the right decision for all of them.

At last they were at the summit. They moved off to the side on one of the platforms where it was just the two of them. Niko stood next to Sofia. The view was stunning. There was so much to take in, from the lighthouse below them to Waikiki Beach off in the distance.

"Isn't this the most amazing thing you've ever seen?" Sofia smiled as she gazed around.

"Yes, it is." But he was no longer looking at the view. He was looking at her. The wind swept through the short strands of her hair as a smile lit up her whole face. She'd never looked more beautiful.

This was it.

This was his prime opportunity to keep Sofia in his life. His plan just had to work. By now she had to know just how good they could be together.

When Sofia glanced over at him, her cheeks grew rosy. "You're supposed to be taking in the view. That's why we hiked all the way up here."

"I am taking in the view. And it's gorgeous."

"Niko. You're being impossible."

"No. I'm just being honest." Was that a bit of color in her cheeks? Had he made her blush?

She smiled and shook her head. "You best look around *at the scenery* because we can't stay up here forever. Other people will want this spot."

"They can wait for a bit." Long enough for him to make the biggest, most important proposal of his life.

Sofia arched a brow. "Niko, what's up with you?"

He drew on scenes in movies to figure out how exactly to go about this correctly. He was supposed to drop down on one knee. He could do that. Down he went on bended knee.

Sofia's mouth gaped, but no words came out. She pressed a hand to her mouth.

This was it. His big moment. "Sofia, I've been trying to figure out a solution to our problem, and at last I know the answer. Marry me?" When she still didn't say anything, but continued to stare at him, he added, "We make a great team. We can do this for our child."

The surprise faded from her face and was replaced by an expression he couldn't quite read. For a moment, nothing could be heard but the rustling of the wind. Why wasn't she saying anything? Did she understand this was the best solution for all of them? Somehow they'd make it work...for their child.

"No."

Surely he hadn't heard her correctly. Then, realizing that he'd forgotten the most important part of the proposal, he said, "If it's the ring, I promise to get you one when we get back to civilization."

She blinked repeatedly and shook her head. "I can't marry you."

And then she rushed past him toward the pathway, the one they'd just come up. She was leaving him there on bended knee.

This would be his first and last proposal. The memory of her so readily shooting him down was like a big kick in the gut. He refused to ever put himself in that position again.

And try as he might, he couldn't figure out why she'd turned him down. She had to see they made a great team. He got to his feet and turned to witness her hasty exit. It was then he realized a small crowd had formed. Their cell phone cameras were aimed at him.

Niko inwardly groaned. His most humiliating moment would be loaded onto the internet for all the world to see. It wouldn't be long before he went from the poor slob who'd been turned down to the rejected Greek billionaire. Where had he gone wrong?

Not about to stand there for any more photo ops, he set off after her. Did she realize who she'd turned down? The heir to the Stravos fortune. The father to her baby. How could she turn him down? Any other woman would have jumped at his offer.

Then again, Sofia wasn't any other woman. If she was, he probably wouldn't have made the offer. There was most definitely something special about Sofia. Or at least he'd thought so until just a minute ago. His steps slowed. Why should he chase after her when she'd made her feelings so clear?

She moved swiftly down the steps and through the little tunnel. He didn't push himself to catch up with her. In fact, he purposely lingered in the background. It was probably best he kept a little distance. The more time that passed, the more her rejection stung.

He'd never understand women. They continued to be an utter mystery to him. And he had no idea where he and Sofia went from here.

What's wrong with me?

Any other woman would have jumped at the offer to marry a billionaire. And it wouldn't matter the circumstances.

Why did she have to be the exception? Why couldn't she just make do with what Niko was offering her?

A life of luxury.

She could have anything her heart desired and visit far-flung places, things that would forever be out of her reach otherwise. It would be a dream come true for most people. Just not her. Was it wrong that she longed for more?

After they'd made love beneath the sun, she'd been sure it would make a profound difference in their relationship. But the words of love never came from Niko. It was as though he wanted to get close to her, but not too close. This realization made her heart sink.

Now back at the hotel suite, Sofia paused from

wiping down the kitchen counter—the last room to be cleaned. The place was eerily silent without Niko around. The hour was growing quite late. She moved to the picture window that overlooked the ocean as the moonlight danced on the water. Where could he be?

She hadn't laid eyes on him since he'd dropped her off after their visit to Diamond Head. She tried to recall everything that had been said at the summit, but it was all a blur.

The truth of the matter was she'd never expected his proposal. There had been no telltale signs. No sense that he was about to pop the question. One minute they'd been having a good time together, and the next he was down on one knee.

For a moment, her heart had been in her throat. She thought all her dreams were about to come true. And then he'd opened his mouth and spouted out what sounded like a business negotiation. Not a romantic proposal founded in love. The backs of her eyes stung with unshed tears. *Darn hormones.*

When they'd arrived back at the Stravos Star Hotel, he hadn't even gotten out of the car. The only words he'd spoken to her were to tell her to get her things packed.

It didn't come as any surprise. What remained

to be seen was whether he'd have her booked onto a commercial airliner or whether he'd fly her back to New York on his jet. Why bother waiting when she could make the arrangements herself?

She moved to the couch where she'd left her laptop. Somehow the thought of being back in New York City didn't bring her the comfort she'd hoped it would. Her fingers moved over the keyboard. Oh, well, that really didn't matter at this point. She had to get on with her life.

The front door opened, and footsteps could be heard in the entryway. Sofia steeled herself, ready to deal with Niko's anger. After all, she had turned him down without any explanation. But what could she say? She refused to admit that she'd been waiting for a heartfelt proposal.

Niko's eyes widened when he found her sitting cross-legged at the end of the couch. "I didn't think you'd still be awake."

Countless responses came to her mind from sarcastic to sincere, but what passed her lips surprised even her. "Can I get you something to eat? There are some leftovers in the fridge."

He set his car keys down on the breakfast nook. "I'm not hungry. I'm going to bed."

When he started toward his room, Sofia called

out to him. "Niko, wait." He paused but he didn't face her. *Fine.* At least he was listening. "We need to talk."

He turned around. His eyes were icy cold. "Do you want to explain why you turned me down? Because I don't get it. Was it because I didn't have a diamond ring?"

She shook her head. "It had nothing to do with the ring."

"You know I would have gotten you one. The biggest and best."

She didn't doubt that. After all, he was a Stravos. They were known for their fine taste. "It was nothing like that."

"Then I don't understand. I thought we were having a good time. Not to mention you're having my baby. The next logical step would be for us to get married. Isn't that what you wanted? What you've been waiting for?"

"No! That isn't what I've been waiting for. Not at all."

Niko sighed as his fingers forked their way through his hair. "Then I don't understand. What do you want?"

Sofia worried her bottom lip. How did she explain this to him? Didn't he know it took a strong, loving relationship to get through the good and the bad? Money wasn't a substitute. It wasn't even close.

At last she realized there was no way to say it nicely—to try to preserve his feelings. If he wanted the truth, she owed him that much. "I don't want you proposing to me out of obligation. That's not good enough—"

"I'm beginning to wonder if anything will be enough for you."

"Hey! That's not fair."

"And you think getting turned down in front of a crowd is fair."

"I...I didn't ask you to propose. I didn't even hint at it."

Lines formed between his dark brows. "You're right. You didn't. I thought I was doing the right thing." He swore under his breath. "I've given this a lot of thought, and it makes sense. You're just too stubborn to see it."

"I am not."

"You know what? This conversation is a waste of time. You're going to marry me. And all three of us are going to be a family."

Sofia shook her head. "Baby or no baby, you're *not* going to dictate to me what I do. I am *not* marrying you."

His lips pressed into a firm line as his eyes darkened. Was that anger lurking in his gaze? Or was it pain? She couldn't tell. And at that particular moment, she didn't care.

"The suite is now clean. My bags are packed. I'll be ready to leave in the morning." Afraid this conversation was about to take a really bad turn, she set off for her room. With long, sure strides, she reached it in no time and slammed her door shut.

There was no way Niko or any man was going to tell her when or who she'd marry. *How dare he!* She was not an obligation that needed tending to. She was a woman who wanted to be loved and cherished. Was that asking too much?

She thought of her parents. Raising five children, they'd had their share of tough times, but somehow they'd stuck it out. And there were times when it would have been easier to just quit. But they never did. Through thick and thin, they held on. They couldn't have done that without a deep, abiding love for each other.

And that was what Sofia wanted. A man who would love her no matter what. She refused to settle for less. Even if that meant being a single parent and growing old alone.

CHAPTER SIXTEEN

TALK ABOUT AWKWARD. This is downright impossible.

Niko glanced over his laptop at Sofia. She sat across the aisle and continued to stare out the plane's window as though mesmerized by the blue skies and passing fluffy white clouds. He knew she was upset with him. He'd really botched everything.

The truth of the matter was he may have had his share of dates, but that's all they were—casual affairs. He knew nothing about relationships and making women happy. And with his grandfather gone, he had no one he was comfortable going to for such intimate advice.

Sofia had barely spoken more than two words to him since their argument last night. He had the feeling she was waiting for him to apologize, but his wounded ego wasn't so willing.

"Is there something you need?"

Her voice drew him from his thoughts. He cleared his throat. "What did you say?"

"You're staring at me, so I was wondering if you need something. Maybe you have some more spreadsheet work for me to do. If so, I'd like to get started." Her tone lacked emotion. It was as though their relationship had been reduced to nothing more than coworkers on a business trip.

"Um...no. I don't have anything for you to work on."

Her gaze moved from him to the mess of papers on the seat next to him. Okay, so maybe he could use a hand, but he wasn't ready to act as if nothing had happened between them. Not sure what to say to her at this point, he turned back to his laptop and started typing again.

"You're going to have to talk to me sooner or later."

He glanced at her over the monitor of his laptop again. "We don't have anything to discuss. You made that quite clear yesterday at Diamond Head."

"I tried to talk to you last night, but you weren't in any mood to hear me out."

"And you think I'm in a better mood today?" After a night of tossing and turning, he was exhausted. The truth of the matter was that while the rest of the world was in dreamland, he'd realized he'd been wrong. He'd just sprung the proposal on her, and that hadn't been fair. But did she have to shut him down so coldly and walk away without an explanation?

"I just think if we talk things out we don't have to part as enemies. After all, we're having a baby."

She was right. For the baby's sake, they needed to make peace with each other. But was that even possible? There was a spot in his chest that ached every time he recalled her turning down his marriage proposal.

He swallowed hard. "What's there to discuss? You turned me down. Plain and simple. There's even a video circulating on the internet of the event just in case I don't remember it clearly enough."

"What?" Sofia's jaw dropped. "But why? Who would post something like that?"

"Apparently a billionaire getting turned down is an internet sensation. At last count, it was over a million views."

"But surely we can have it taken down. That's not right. It was supposed to be a private moment between the two of us."

"In this day of technology, it would appear nothing is private." Niko closed his laptop and set it aside. "What I still don't understand is why you turned me down."

"I already told you. I don't want you proposing out of obligation."

"But what about providing a family for our baby? Isn't that important, too?" He needed to make her see that she was wrong—that she'd made a mistake by turning down his well-thought-out offer. "And what about financial security? You'd never have to worry about money again."

She shook her head. "There's more to life than money."

"I know that." He'd learned a lot since spending time with Sofia—obviously not quite enough. He shrugged. "What do you want me to say? You want something from me that I'm obviously unable to give you."

"Are you sure about that?" Her gaze needled him as though searching for the truth.

"Listen, I gave it my best shot."

Sofia reached across the aisle, grasping his forearm and squeezing it. "I'm not trying to hurt you. It's just that maybe when you do find the right woman, you'll know not to make the same mistakes."

Mistakes? He pulled away from her touch. He was Nikolas Stravos III. He didn't make mistakes. His grandfather raised him to always do his best—to be flawless. Oh, who was he kidding? He'd blown this whole thing royally.

If he hadn't gotten excited and rushed things, he could have pulled it off. He could have had the flowers, a candlelit dinner, some mood music and whatever else went into a fancy evening. He mentally kicked himself for messing up this bad. Thank goodness his grandfather wasn't around to admonish him for rushing and not doing his due diligence.

He glanced across the aisle as Sofia fidgeted with her phone. He knew he was letting his pride get in the way. This was the time when he needed to be a bigger man—for his child's sake. Wasn't that what a good parent would do?

Niko choked down his pride. It was time to do the right thing. "I'm sorry."

Sofia's head lifted, and her startled gaze met his. Was it so strange to hear him apologize? If so, then perhaps he did have to make some changes.

"Apology accepted. Do you know how long it'll be until we're in New York?"

New York? Was that where she thought they were headed? Their trip wasn't over…not yet. He had a little more time to get this thing between them right.

"We won't be in New York for a few more days."

"Days? But I thought…" Her lips pressed together as though she were weighing her next words. "I just thought after everything that happened—"

"That I'd be anxious to get rid of you?"

She shrugged. "Something like that."

He couldn't help but shake his head. Here he was thinking that somehow, someway he could find a way to keep her in his life, and there she was thinking he wanted to get rid of her, the sooner, the better.

Maybe it was best they got back to their working relationship. "We still have an agreement, and not all of the suites have been closed. Unless you've changed your mind."

She hesitated. He willed her to stick out the trip until the end. He thought of sweetening the deal to entice her to stay on, but his pride held him back. If she continued on, he wanted it to be her choice—free and clear.

"I haven't changed my mind."

"Good." Niko shifted his attention back to transferring his grandfather's handwritten ledger sheets to the computer.

"Can I help?"

Niko glanced up, meeting Sofia's warm brown eyes. His heart slammed into his ribs, and he had the sudden urge to sweep her into his arms and kiss away her doubts about them. But he knew that would only exacerbate their issues.

Instead, he handed over some raw data and showed her where to find the databases that needed populating. He also told her what reports needed to be generated when she was done.

In an effort to keep from giving in to his desires to feel her lips against his, he began organizing the papers he'd discarded haphazardly during his foul mood. Things still weren't back to normal between them, but at least they were on speaking terms. He'd take that as a good sign.

He cast Sofia a sideways glance. As though she sensed him staring at her again, she glanced over. Was that a smile tugging at her lips? Or was he just looking for any sign of encouragement?

"Did you need something else?"

"No. Did I give you everything you need?"

"I think so." She fingered her way through the pages. "It looks like it."

"All right. I'll just put the rest of these away." He started closing files and inserting them in his briefcase, when he stumbled across a blue scrapbook from the Honolulu suite.

Niko had retrieved it from the safe as soon as they had arrived, but then he'd had a meeting, followed by Sofia's slip and fall. He'd been so distracted that he'd forgotten all about it. There were no words or pictures on the outside to indicate what he might find between the covers.

He undid the gold string holding the book closed and flipped open the cover. Inside he found a baby picture with his full name and statistics listed beneath it. The curvy print was familiar to him—it was his mother's handwriting.

Niko turned the page, finding a tiny bracelet with his name on it as well as the name of the hospital glued to the page. Next to it was a photo of his mother cradling him in her arms. There was a note next to the picture: *I never knew so much love could come in such a small package.*

Niko's eyes misted up, and he blinked repeatedly. He continued turning pages, learning about his first steps and his first word: *Dada*. And there were finger paintings from preschool.

When he stumbled across a handwritten letter, it drew him in for a close look. Again, it was his mother's handwriting.

Niko,

You caught us by surprise. I must admit that I was a nervous wreck when I found out I was pregnant with you. I had no idea how to be a mother, but your father was a rock. I leaned on him, and he leaned back. We helped each other through the tough parts, and together we celebrated the miracle that had come into our lives—you.

And now that you're here, our family is complete. Each day I watch you grow, and you amaze me with your fearless approach to life. I hope you never lose that sense of adventure, even when new things make you hesitate. Just keep putting one foot in front of the other. It will work out in the end.

I look forward to watching you grow into a strong man like your father. But never be afraid to listen to your heart. It will set you

*apart from the others. Use it as your compass
in life, keeping you honest and happy.*

*I am so honored to be your mother and to
call you my son. Remember that your father
and I will always love you, no matter what.*
I love you very much,
Mom

Niko's eyesight blurred. He ran the backs of his
hands over his eyes as he swallowed the lump
in his throat. This scrapbook meant the world to
him. In fact, he planned to make a similar one
for his child.

He glanced over at Sofia. She appeared absorbed
in her work. Her brow was drawn, and her bottom
lip was between her teeth. It was something she
did when she was deep in thought. He couldn't
help but smile. She was totally adorable. He didn't
think he'd ever get tired of staring at her.

He went back to the scrapbook, but as he turned
the page it was blank. He continued turning the
pages until the very end, hoping to find some
more snippets of his past, but there were no more.
His mother hadn't had an opportunity to fill in
the other highlights of his life. She'd been stolen
away far too soon.

It was as though his family knew what was going on in his life as far as Sofia and the baby were concerned. It was as if they were sending him helpful hints. Niko had never believed in signs before, but his grandfather had definitely meant to teach him something about life on this trip. Did his grandfather have any idea just how timely his lesson would be?

Niko knew once he let go of this chance to be happy with Sofia that he'd never get it back. He didn't know exactly how to keep her in his life, but he had to try something different—something more enticing.

CHAPTER SEVENTEEN

DID NIKO HAVE another adventure in mind?

Once their plane touched down in New Orleans, Sofia thought they'd be going directly to the Stravos Star Hotel. But instead the limo delivered them to the French Quarter.

As she followed him out of the car, the heat surprised her. For some reason, she thought with it being September the temperature would have dropped, but not in New Orleans. The warm breeze and humidity made it feel as though it was still summertime.

"Niko, what are we doing here?" He'd been acting suspicious ever since they'd arrived. He'd been on his phone and speaking in whispered tones.

"You'll find out soon."

With anyone else this bit of mystery would worry her, but during the time she'd spent with Niko, she'd come to trust him. Still, she couldn't imagine what had him so excited. The *clip-clop* of hooves drew her attention. She glanced down the street to find a fine white horse pulling a gleaming white carriage. It stopped in front of them. *What in the world?*

"Your carriage, madam." Niko waved his hand toward the carriage.

"Are you serious?"

"Of course I am. You said you've never been to New Orleans before, and I didn't want to rush in and out of town without giving you the grand tour."

"Really?" When he nodded, she continued, "Can we see Bourbon Street? The wax museum? Mardi Gras World? Oh, and maybe visit a steamboat—"

"Slow down. Where in the world did you come up with all of that?"

"Hey, you aren't the only one who knows how to surf the internet. While you were on the phone at the airport, I was researching the city. There's so much to do here."

He smiled as he helped her into the carriage. He took the seat opposite her, and they set off on their adventure. "You know, to squeeze everything in that you want to do, we might have to stay for a couple of days."

She shrugged, trying to act casual. Yet inside

she was now the one who was excited. This city was full of energy, and she couldn't wait to go exploring. "It's okay. We don't have to stay. I know we have to keep moving—"

"I think we can make the time for some sight-seeing."

"You do?" Her words were rushed as heat warmed her cheeks.

He nodded. "Just let me know if there are any other sights you'd like to visit."

She agreed as she sat back in her seat, taking in the colorful buildings lining the street. Even though she'd grown up in New York City, she'd never gone for a horse and carriage ride in Central Park. So this was a real treat for her.

As they turned a corner, the scent of Creole food wafted through the air. Sofia inhaled deeply just as her stomach growled. She sure hoped Niko would be up for trying some of the local cuisine.

A little ways into the ride, he moved to the seat next to her. The carriage wasn't all that big, so their arms and thighs brushed. Her heart picked up its pace. She willed it to remain calm, but that was impossible with Niko so close by. If she were to turn her head ever so slightly, they'd be face-to-face, lip to lip.

She remained facing forward, resisting the temptation. "Something wrong with your seat?"

"Yes. It's all the way over there."

The playful tone of his voice was yet another ding to her defenses. She tried to sound serious. "Did you need something?"

"For you to talk to me."

"I am talking to you."

"No. I mean I want us to be friends again."

How could she not be friends with him? He was the father of her baby and...and she truly cared about him. More than she wanted to let on even to herself.

She clasped her hands in her lap. "Who said we weren't friends?"

"Don't pretend like I didn't mess things up with that marriage proposal. We were getting along great, and then I thought I knew what was best. I'm sorry."

"Apology accepted. And I'm sorry I didn't respond better. You caught me off guard."

"It would appear I have much to learn about relationships."

"You and me both. I thought I had a clue with my ex, but I was so wrong." As she contemplated her next words, her heart pounded loudly in her chest, keeping time with the horse's hooves. "In a relationship, both people have to want the same things and…and feel the same way about each other."

There, she'd said it. She glanced away and stared out at the passing buildings and pedestrians. What he'd do with the information, she didn't know.

"Maybe we can learn together."

She turned to him, catching a gleam of desire in his eyes. "Niko, what do you have in mind?"

"Once we get to the hotel, you could teach me a thing or two. And I could show you what I know."

Leave it to Niko to turn an apology into an opportunity for flirting. She wondered if he knew how tempting she found his idea.

No matter how hard she fought it, this guy got to her on a totally different level than anyone else she'd ever known had. He was in her mind, her blood and her heart. *Whoa!* Did she just mention Niko and her heart in the same sentence?

When he leaned forward, she didn't back away. She knew he was going to kiss her, and in that moment, she couldn't think of any reason to pull away. She wanted him, too. Maybe it was just a fantasy that he could ever feel the same way about her, but what would it hurt to pretend just a little longer?

His lips pressed to hers, causing her heart to thump loudly in her ears. His fingers brushed along her cheek. As their kiss deepened, a moan swelled in her throat. It felt like forever since they'd kissed. So much had changed. And somehow even though they'd been driven apart, she'd never felt closer to him. She knew it didn't make any sense, and maybe just for this moment that was all right.

Much too soon the carriage rolled to a stop. Regretfully, Sofia pulled back. Trying to act as if Niko hadn't just totally rocked her world right off its axis, she glanced around. "Where are we?"

"Jackson Square. It's a mix of history and culture. I thought you might like it."

She was intrigued. A small street band filled the air with jazz tunes. Sofia resisted the urge to hum along with the saxophone. They certainly knew how to live down here.

A wrought iron fence surrounded the square with artists and their colorful work along the perimeter. "Do we have time to look around?"

"Certainly. That's why we're here."

Anxious to see absolutely everything, she set off at a brisk pace. Her hand was seized by Niko's much larger hand. His fingers laced through hers.

"Slow down." He leaned in close. "I don't want you getting away."

She didn't think that was possible—not that she had any desire to escape his presence. She glanced over to give him a reassuring smile, and then her gaze landed on his lips. Well, she did have some desires pulsating through her veins, but she suppressed them.

She didn't want to give Niko the wrong idea. Things couldn't return to the way they'd been on that deserted island in Hawaii.

She hadn't changed her mind about his marriage proposal. When she married it would be for love, not to make life more convenient.

They meandered around, taking in the numerous artists and their varying styles. Sofia loved the bright, cheery colors. The numerous canvases had images that ranged from a sax with drums to historic buildings in the French Quarter to a streetcar. They were all vibrant, just the like the city itself.

As Sofia passed in front of the gates leading to the park, she spotted a beautiful fountain and a statue of Andrew Jackson astride a horse. She'd explore it later. Right now, she was more interested in the beautiful and eclectic artwork. She was truly tempted to purchase a piece of art for her new home in New York—a reminder of this magical trip.

When they happened on an older man in a sunny-yellow T-shirt and faded denim overalls splattered in paint, he waved them over. On the railing behind him were sketches. "Have a seat? Let me sketch you."

Sofia ran a hand over her short hair, knowing with all the traveling that day she didn't look her best. "Thanks. But I don't think so."

"Go ahead," Niko encouraged. "Don't you want a souvenir from our trip?"

Yet again it was as if he'd been reading her thoughts. "I have some from Hawaii."

"Ah, but you don't have any from the French Quarter."

And then she had an idea. "I'll pose if you do, too."

"I don't know if we have time for all of that."

"I'm fast." The artist smiled broadly.

Niko's gaze moved back from the man to Sofia. "That's not fair with both of you ganging up on me."

"Oh, please." Sofia pleaded with her eyes.

"Okay, but you go first."

"You don't understand. I want you to be sketched with me. It'll be for our baby." She just knew that Niko wouldn't be able to turn her down now.

And she was right. The artist set up another folding chair next to hers. With Niko's body pressed up beside hers and his arm draped over her shoulder, their image was sketched. She'd never admit it to Niko, but she wanted this drawing for herself—to remember this happy moment. Because all too soon he'd be halfway around the globe from her running his empire.

The next evening Niko sat next to Sofia on the jet bound for the Caribbean. It was to be their last stop before heading north to New York. Guilt weighed on him. He'd promised Sofia a memorable stay in New Orleans, but aside from that one kiss he'd stolen in the carriage, Sofia had kept him at arm's length.

He'd hoped with time she'd let down her guard, but that morning they'd been alerted to a storm coming in off the Gulf. He'd helped her, and they'd closed the suite in record time.

"I'm really sorry about this." He hoped she believed him.

Sofia's eyes widened in surprise. "You're apologizing for an approaching tropical storm with the potential to turn into a hurricane. What were you supposed to do? I know you're rich and powerful, but even you aren't any match for a storm that size. And don't forget that it had New Orleans in its crosshairs."

"Yes, but I promised we could do whatever your heart desired. I know—I'll take you back whenever you want."

"So if I said I want to go back next month, you'd just drop everything, jump on your jet and fly to the States to take me on vacation?"

"Yes." He said it without any hesitation, and the ease of his response combined with his utter honesty surprised even him.

She smiled. "Be careful or I might start believing you."

This was his moment to ask for a second chance.

"Sofia, we're good together. What can I do to get you to reconsider my proposal?"

She shook her head. "Nothing. It's better this way."

Frustration pumped through his veins, but he forced his voice to remain neutral. "How do you get that?"

"Because all of this—" she waved her hand around at the luxurious cabin "—is nothing more than a fantasy. Once we return to our normal lives, reality will set in. We're from very diverse worlds with different expectations."

"But what we shared on this trip is a starting place—a foundation. We can build on it."

She shook her head again. "It won't work."

Niko's fingers tightened around the armrests. "Why do you have to be so stubborn?"

"Because I believed in forever once. And…"

"And?" Niko couldn't let her stop there. He had to know exactly what he was up against.

"And I found out that I was wrong. I thought I could change Bobby, and he thought he could change me. We both failed. I failed. I won't put myself through that again. I like who I am. I don't want to change into a person I don't recognize just to try and be what someone wants me to be."

Niko sat forward in his seat so he could look her directly in the eyes. "I may mess up from time to time, but I'll never intentionally hurt you. And I think you're wonderful just the way you are." He smiled at her, trying to lighten the mood. "Maybe a bit too stubborn—"

"Ha! Listen to who's talking. You have stubbornness down to a fine art."

He couldn't argue. "But I'm serious. We could be a family for our child."

"What if...if later on you decide you're tired of playing family man and look elsewhere for fun?"

"Is that what happened with your ex?"

She nodded. "I caught him in our bed with someone else."

Niko swore under his breath. "I promise I'll never do that to you. First of all, I can't imagine ever getting bored of you and looking elsewhere. And secondly, if we didn't work out, I'd tell you straight up. There wouldn't be any guessing. I respect you too much to sneak behind your back."

She stared at him for a moment as though trying to decide if she believed him. "I don't know what to think right now."

"That's okay. Just relax. You don't have to decide anything right now. I want you to enjoy our visit in the Caribbean. Okay?"

She nodded. "I've never been there."

"Neither have I. At least not that I can remember. So we'll experience it together. Would you like that?"

"I would."

He reached out and took her hand in his. She hadn't said it outright, but this was his second chance. And he intended to take full advantage of it.

There had to be a way to convince her that he wasn't like her ex—but how? Especially since he'd already messed up the proposal. Niko was smart enough not to make the same mistake twice.

CHAPTER EIGHTEEN

THIS WAS AN ISLAND?

Sofia stared out the windshield at the passing green foliage. For some reason, she'd been thinking the Caribbean islands would be all beaches and sun. But this elevated area was lush with bushes, palms and flowers. It was definitely paradise—just different from what she'd pictured in her mind.

"Do you know where we're going?" She hadn't seen any buildings for a while now, and the vegetation was growing denser.

"Are you getting worried?" Niko glanced at her.

"You're following the GPS on your phone, aren't you?"

"It doesn't work out here."

"What? Are you serious?" *Say it isn't so.*

"Relax. I know exactly where we're going."

"How? Did you get directions back at the airport?" *Please, oh, please say you did.* But if he was the least bit like her father, then she knew the answer—he hadn't.

Niko just smiled at her. "You don't think I can get us there, do you?"

Did he really want her to answer that question? She knew he wouldn't like her answer. Instead she asked, "Shouldn't we be down by the beach?"

"You'd think so, but apparently my family wanted something different." He navigated the open-top, cherry-red Jeep down a narrow dirt lane. "Come on. Admit it. You think I'll get us lost."

The denial stuck in the back of her throat. She just couldn't get the words out. When it came to her experience with men and directions, well, the cards were stacked against Niko.

He stomped on the brakes and turned to her. "Come on. You can say it."

"I...I think you should turn around before we end up utterly lost." She pulled out her phone to see if there was any cell service. There wasn't so much as a flicker of a bar.

Her body tensed as she glanced around. Did that shrub just move? Sofia leaned forward, anxious to find out what else was out here in the wilderness with her. If it was some sort of reptile—she inwardly cringed—she would be jumping on Niko's lap. Goose bumps marched up her arms. *Let it be anything but a snake.* In this open-air vehicle, there was no safe place to go. Why did they have to rent a Jeep?

"How about we make a bet?"

He wanted to play games now? Sofia groaned. Set to grouch at him to step on the gas, she hesitated. It might just be easier to placate him. "What are we betting?"

His eyes lit up as though he loved a challenge. "How about we bet on tonight's dinner? If I get us to our destination without getting us lost, you make dinner? But if I get lost, then I'll make dinner?"

She wasn't so sure there would be any winning where this bet was concerned. If they got lost, they'd probably run out of gas and be left to walk out of here. And whatever was causing that bush to periodically shake would eventually come out. She wrung her hands together.

Not wanting to sit there any longer, she glanced over her shoulder at the crate of groceries in the backseat. "Fine. It's a bet."

Niko drove another hundred yards and then turned right into a clearing. In no time, a white villa with a red-tiled roof and green shutters appeared. The whole way around the perimeter was a wide veranda, just perfect for kicking back to sip an iced tea while reading a book. The villa was perched on a hillside, and it provided a sweeping view of the beach and blue waters of the Caribbean.

Relief flooded her body, and her muscles eased. Thank goodness they hadn't gotten lost. Instead, they'd ended up in this little slice of paradise. Maybe Niko wasn't so bad with directions, after all. Then suspicion set in.

Her narrowed gaze settled on Niko. "I smell a rat."

"A rat?" He chuckled." I don't think so. There are no rats here. Just a devastatingly handsome Greek businessman."

"Oh, you." She lightly swiped at his arm. He wasn't getting off that easily. "You knew exactly where we were when you made that bet. You just wanted to get out of cooking. That's cheating."

"No, my dear. That's called betting on a sure thing." He winked at her and then eased the Jeep along the drive to the front of the villa. "Well, now I understand why I never saw any listing in the Stravos Star Hotel papers for a property in the Caribbean."

"I take it this is your family's private residence?"

"So private that I didn't even know it existed." He continued staring at the modest structure as though searching his memory for some mention of it.

"I'm guessing this is different from your home in Greece."

He was no longer smiling as he nodded. "I didn't think it'd be so isolated."

"What's the matter? You afraid a croc might get you?" she teased, hoping to put the smile back on his handsome face.

"Not hardly. But I am worried about the proposal for the shipping line. After convincing my experts that my plan to expand the shipping segment had merit, I set a new deadline for them to formulate their thoughts. It's tomorrow. But I seriously doubt this place has internet access."

"Oh." She wasn't quite sure what to say. And there was no way she could fix the situation. They were in fact in a remote area.

And then she realized that for the first time on this trip, she was totally isolated with Niko. There were no tourists, no staff, no nothing...except a snake or a crocodile.

She glanced around at the wide expanse of trimmed grass. She highly doubted any creature would willingly come out in the wide open. She hoped. The only thing she had to worry about now was the very sexy man sitting next to her. All it would take would be one kiss for her to forget her common sense.

The villa was definitely small by Stravos standards.

While Sofia enjoyed an afternoon nap, Niko decided to explore the house. His bare feet moved soundlessly over the wood floors. Each room had vaulted ceilings with a paddle fan. He made quick work of looking around two of the three bedrooms. Each had cream walls, potted palms, a colorful comforter giving it an island feel and glass doors that opened onto the veranda. All three bathrooms had skylights. An eat-in kitchen came furnished with modern appliances, and a spacious living room looked as though someone still lived here. It was really quite cozy.

Niko found this quaint house more appealing than his spacious island home. This place had a warmth to it. He wasn't quite able to put a name on it. Whatever it was, he immediately felt at home.

In the colorful kitchen, he found the cabinets fully stocked. And there wasn't a bit of dust anywhere. Either interlopers had moved in, or his grandfather had caretakers on retainer. Niko didn't understand why his grandfather had held on to this property—a place they'd never visited.

In the living room, Niko swung open the glass doors, letting in a warm breeze. He turned around to find the room filled with pictures. Some were hanging on the wall. Some were on the shelves. He approached them to have a closer look. He picked up a frame, and there smiling back at him was himself at a very young age. He couldn't have been more than two. Holding him was his father and standing next to them beaming warmly was his mother.

Niko didn't know how much time passed as he examined all the photos in the room. Each appeared to have been taken here on the island.

Then he took in the shelves. Most of the books appeared to be action/adventure titles, but a few were romances. He ran his fingers over the spines. Then he heard footsteps behind him.

He turned to her, unable to find the right words

to describe what he was feeling at the moment—being in this house with his parents' mementos and having Sofia next to him. He'd never felt this way in his life. It was as though everything was at last right in the world.

Between the photos from Tokyo and the scrapbook including the letter from his mother, Niko felt as if the blank parts of his life were being colored in. In New Orleans, they'd recovered a photo album of his father's life, from his baby pictures through to Niko's parents' wedding. There was even a photo of his grandfather playing in the sand with Niko's father.

In the photos, there were so many smiling, laughing faces. Niko had only ever known his grandfather as a man who was reserved and set in his ways. Part of Niko was sad he'd never known that fun side of his grandfather, and another part wondered if Niko was about to miss out on the best time of his life. His chance to play in the sand, so to speak.

As Sofia had pointed out, the photos his grandfather had left him weren't so bad. They had actually answered many questions, some Niko didn't even know that he had. But somehow he felt his grandfather had bigger things in mind. He hadn't been a man to be subtle when a grand gesture would work. But what could it be?

"What have you been up to?" There was still a sleepy tone to her voice.

He turned around and smiled at her. "I was just exploring. I had no idea my parents brought me here when I wasn't much more than a baby."

Sofia glanced around at the pictures. "And a cute baby at that. Do you think our baby will be as cute?"

"Sure. If he's lucky."

"You've never been accused of being modest, have you?"

He sent her a playful smile. "No. But if our child is smart, they'll take their looks off their mom."

She smiled back at him. "Much better, Mr. Stravos."

"I thought you might like that." He loved making her smile. He loved it more than plotting and planning the growth of his shipping empire. "Anything special you'd like to do while we're here?"

She shrugged. "I can't think of anything."

"We could go sightseeing or shopping in the village." When she shook her head, he started to worry. "What about taking a boat tour of the islands?"

"I don't think so." She moved about the living room, examining all the photos. "I need to get back to New York. I've found some apartments that I want to see. I have an appointment for the day after tomorrow. Will that be a problem?"

The day after tomorrow. Less than forty-eight hours and she'd disappear from his life as quickly as she'd entered it. "Niko, if that's a problem, let me know. I'll try to reschedule the viewings. Or I could catch a commercial flight—"

"No." His voice came out much harsher than he'd intended. Her eyes flashed with surprise, and he immediately regretted it. "I mean, it's not necessary. I'll see that you get back in time."

"Thank you." She picked up a photo of him as a baby. "What will you do with this place? I take it that it's not part of your deal with Cristo."

He didn't want to talk about business. He wanted to know why Sofia wasn't interested in doing anything with him. After all, this was their last stop before New York, before Niko returned Sofia to her family—her big, loving family.

"Niko?"

Oh, yes. Her question. "I don't think I'll part with this place. It was obviously very special to my parents. And I feel at home here."

Sofia smiled. "That's good. See—something else has come of this trip. You've found a piece of your past—a piece you didn't even know was missing. Maybe someday you can bring your family here."

She talked as though she didn't plan to be part of that family. And he had absolutely no idea how to change her mind. He needed more time, but he realized he had no legitimate reason to linger on the island. And by the time they reached New York, any chance he had of making a lasting, tangible relationship with Sofia would be gone.

She glanced at the clock on the wall. "I'm going to start dinner. Since we had an early lunch, I'm hungry."

"Would you like some help?"

Her eyes widened. "What about the bet?"

"What bet? I don't recall one."

She laughed and shook her head. "You know, I think this is the beginning of a long friendship." She turned toward the kitchen. "Come on."

He followed her, all the while thinking what it'd be like if they maintained this friendship, but he knew the distance would take its toll. It'd soon deteriorate to emailing photos in between periodic visits. It'd be all about their child, not them.

And the more time he spent with Sofia, the more he realized just how special she truly was, from making him laugh to getting him to loosen up and stop taking life so seriously.

And then a thought struck him. Maybe getting married didn't have to be an obligation—not when you were marrying your best friend.

CHAPTER NINETEEN

THE NEXT MORNING, he awoke before Sofia. The truth of the matter was he hadn't slept well at all, only catching snippets of sleep here and there. How could this place be kept so up-to-date and yet lack an internet hookup? He had so much riding on his proposal to expand the cargo shipping line and yet he was left with nothing but a landline to connect with his office.

As the coffee brewed, the sun crept up over the horizon. Niko's thoughts turned to Sofia. With each passing day, she grew more beautiful. Perhaps it was the glow of motherhood. And with each passing hour, he realized he was that much closer to losing her.

He latched on to a last desperate thought—his grandfather had left him a sort of life lesson at each stop. He wondered what his grandfather had left him here. And would it be anything to help him realize what he was doing wrong with Sofia?

Niko searched all over the villa for a safe. It

wasn't exactly the sort of home to have a wall safe, but to his surprise, in the last bedroom he found a wall safe behind a mirror. The only problem was his grandfather hadn't left him the code.

Niko tried his grandfather's birthday. Nothing. And then, realizing that this was his parents' special place, he tried each of their birth dates. Nada. Their anniversary. No such luck. Niko groaned. This couldn't be happening.

He refused to give up. There had to be a way into that safe. But trying to locate a safecracker on an island this size would be an impossible task. And he just didn't have the patience to wait for someone to fly in.

In a last-ditch effort, he used his own birth date. The safe snicked open. What he found inside wasn't a stack of photos, but instead bundles of letters. Two to be exact. One was addressed to his mother. And the other stack was addressed to his father.

Intrigued, Niko carried them to the living room. He untied the first bundle. Inside the first envelope he found pictures of his parents' honeymoon right here on this island—in this very house. There were other photos of them dancing beneath the stars and staring at each other as though they were the only two people in the world.

And then Niko unfolded the first letter. It was from his mother to his father. It described the amazing ways his father had swept her off her feet from the bouquet of wildflowers to the walk in the starlight to the amazing meal his father had prepared his mother.

His father could cook? That was news to Niko. It made him wonder if he had some hidden culinary talent. He'd never tried. It was always easier to let the staff handle it or to call room service.

But there was no room service here. And he had picked up a few tips from Sofia the night before. He might be able to tackle something simple—at least to start with.

He continued reading the letters. They were like a detailed how-to dating guide. And though he felt uncomfortable invading his parents' privacy, there really wasn't anything inappropriate in them. They were more about how they had made each other feel and how his father hated leaving his mother for business trips and how he'd make it up to her when he returned. Apparently his mother preferred to spend much of her time right here in this villa versus the grand house on the island in Greece. *Interesting.*

The more Niko read, the more he knew about his parents. It was something he'd craved most of his life. And now at last he felt truly connected to them. And it was thanks to Sofia. Without her, he wouldn't have made it this far in the journey. He'd really thought it was a fool's errand. But now he saw things so differently.

Was it possible that his parents were somehow sending him a message? Was this what he needed to do to sweep Sofia off her feet?

Eager to read it all, he shuffled through the papers. When he came across his parents' marriage license, he paused. They'd been married here on the island. What struck Niko the most was learning that his mother had been pregnant with him when his parents had been married. It was as if his family was speaking to him through this memorabilia his grandfather had preserved for him. Now Niko just had to follow their advice.

Over a candlelit dinner, he'd make it known that he wanted Sofia in his life and it had nothing to do with feeling obligated because of the baby. He wouldn't pressure her about the future. They could just take it one day at a time.

* * *

Sofia couldn't believe how tired she was.

Globe-trotting must take more out of a pregnant person than she'd ever imagined. She'd slept in that morning, and then again this afternoon she'd taken a nap. Niko was going to think she was lazy.

She threw her legs over the edge of the bed and paused. She heard something. Was that music? She listened more closely. It was indeed, and it was a romantic tune. A smile tugged at her lips. Perhaps Niko had learned something about romance, after all. If nothing else, he had good taste in music.

She moved to the bathroom to wash her face and fix her hair when she heard a screeching beep repeatedly go off. Was that a smoke alarm?

Sofia ran to the kitchen, finding smoke rolling through it. Niko took a dish from the oven and rushed to the sink. He placed the smoldering dish in the sink and turned on the water.

Sofia opened all the windows and turned on the overhead paddle fan. When she returned to Niko's side, his face was creased with a deep-set frown.

"What was that?" she asked.

"Your dinner."

"Oh, I see." She didn't, not really. Try as she

might, she just couldn't make out what the charred remains had once been. "What were you trying to make?"

"Fish and vegetables." He raked his fingers through his hair. "I don't know what happened."

She moved to the stove. "Were you supposed to broil it?"

"What?"

She'd never seen him look so unnerved except for that one time in the hospital. "The oven is set on Broil, not Bake."

His frown deepened even more. Then his head lowered, and he shook it. "I ruined everything."

"Ruined what?"

He expelled a deep sigh. "I meant for tonight to be special, what with it being our last night on the island. I was going to cook you dinner and have this nice intimate evening."

"You know what they say, don't you?"

"That I'm an utter failure in the kitchen?"

She couldn't help but smile. "No. That it's the thought that counts."

His gaze met hers. "So you're not mad?"

She shook her head. "I'm impressed that you'd even try. Have you ever cooked before?"

"Never. I found this recipe in one of the drawers and thought I could surprise you."

"You did that all right." She glanced around the kitchen and realized he must have dirtied every dish trying to make her dinner. It was going to take a long time to straighten up the place.

"I know. It looks really bad. Why don't we drive into the village for dinner, and I'll clean this up when we get back?"

She scanned the room again. "I think we better work on it now." She moved to the sink to figure out where to start. "It'll be a million times harder if it dries."

"If you say so, but you're not doing it. Here." He moved to the table and retrieved a bunch of wildflowers. "I picked these for you."

"They're gorgeous. Thank you." There were shades of red, orange, yellow and white. As her nose and eyes grew itchy, she wanted to groan in frustration. But she didn't have the heart to tell him that she was allergic to most wildflowers, not after his dinner disaster. She pretended to inhale their sweet scent, all the while holding her breath and hoping she wouldn't start to sneeze.

"At least I got that part right."

"Yes, you did. Maybe you should put them in

water." She held them out to him and prayed he wouldn't protest. The more distance between her and them, the better.

"Um, sure." He accepted them. "Any idea what I should put them in?"

"If you don't see any vases, I'd use a drinking glass."

He nodded. Something told her this was his first time picking flowers for a woman. She smiled broadly as she headed to the sink and discreetly rubbed her itchy nose. She would not sneeze.

Would. Not. Sneeze.

"Ha-choo!" *Darn it.*

She set to work clearing a side of the sink in order to rinse dishes off before cleaning them. One thing this villa lacked was a dishwasher. She set to work, and Niko was right by her side, doing everything he could to help.

An hour later with the kitchen put to rights, they sat down at the table with a tossed salad and a side of fresh bread that Sofia had thought to pick up in the village earlier that day. Romantic music still played softly in the background.

Sofia couldn't resist adding some candles to the table. Once they were lit, she dimmed the overhead lights. "Is this more what you had in mind?"

At last a smile lifted his lips. "It is."

Niko made small talk about the documents he'd found in the safe. Sofia wasn't the least bit surprised to find that his parents enjoyed spending time here. It was cozy and comfortable. There were no formal airs or luxury furniture that would make anyone nervous they might somehow mar its beauty. This was much closer to what Sofia was used to—except for the view. It was awe inspiring.

"It's a shame you were too young to have memories of the time you spent here with your parents."

"Thanks to you, I have the photos."

"Me?" She set her fork down. "But I didn't have anything to do with it. Your grandfather is the one who orchestrated everything, including the upkeep of this villa."

"But it was you that made me promise to complete this journey. I was really tempted to cut the trip short and let someone else finish closing up the family suites, but you insisted I should see it through. And I thank you. I've learned so much—"

"Ha-choo! Ha-choo!"

Sofia's gaze moved to the beautiful arrangement

of flowers. And then her eyes started to tear up. *Oh, great! Does this have to happen now?*

"Sofia, what is it?"

She shook her head and went in search of some tissues. Once she had her itchy nose under control, she returned to the table.

"You're allergic, aren't you?" Niko's voice held a don't-lie-to-me tone.

She nodded, not wanting to make him feel bad. And then she noticed the flowers had been removed from the table. "I'm sorry."

"You should have told me before."

"I…I didn't want to make you feel bad. I loved the flowers. Honest. It's just that I'm allergic to a lot of them."

"But at the wedding they didn't seem to bother you."

"There are certain flowers that don't bother me, like roses, lilies and orchids."

"Oh. I wish I'd known. I really made a mess of tonight."

The fact he cared this much touched her heart. She knew it would be best not to start up anything romantic on the eve of their departure to New York, but she wasn't ready to say goodbye yet. The burned food, messy kitchen and allergies wouldn't ruin this evening. It was touching to witness Niko going beyond his comfort zone and trying something new just to impress her. It was what a man did for someone he loved.

She got to her feet and held out her hand to him. His gaze moved from her outstretched arm to her eyes. His brows arched. "What do you have in mind?"

"Trust me."

"After what I put you through tonight, you might be ushering me to the veranda to sleep tonight."

She smiled broadly. "If you don't come with me, you might be right."

He jumped to his feet and clasped her hand in his. "Then by all means lead the way."

She grabbed one candle, and he grabbed the other. She led him to the living room, where she dimmed the lights. And then she moved into Niko's arms. Their bodies swayed together. Niko pulled her closer. The soft curves of her breasts pressed to the hard plains of his broad chest. Her head rested against his shoulder, and she inhaled the slightest hint of a spicy cologne. Its heady scent had an intoxicating effect on her.

"I don't want this night to end." Niko's voice was deep and soothing.

Sofia's heart pounded. "Me, either."

"You mean it?" His gaze searched hers.

"I do."

Tonight would be it. This evening would be the beginning of the rest of their lives—together. Because she knew what this whole evening was leading up to—Niko was going to tell her he loved her. At last, her dreams would come true. She would have one of those forever relationships that weathered the good and bad times. Like her parents and her grandparents.

Her hands slid up over his shoulders and stroked the back of his neck. Her heart *thump-thumped* in her chest. She pulled back just enough for her gaze to latch on to his tempting lips. As though he had exactly the same thought, his mouth claimed hers. There was certainty in the kiss. They both knew what they wanted—each other.

Her heart pounded even harder. Her head spun with the most delicious sensations. She planned to make this night last as long as possible. It'd taken them so long to reach this point that it needed to be savored.

Words of love rushed to the back of her throat. She wanted to tell him how she felt, but she couldn't. When he told her he loved her, she needed it to be because that was how he truly felt and not because he was following her lead. She needed the words to come from his heart.

She needed this to be real—to be genuine. For all of their sakes.

CHAPTER TWENTY

EVERY DREAM MUST END. There came a time when everyone had to wake up to the realities of life.

For Sofia, that startling moment came with dawn's early morning rays. After a delicious night of lovemaking, Niko never said a word about loving her. He cared. That was obvious. But Sofia knew it wouldn't be enough, not for the long haul.

She'd had a caring relationship with Bobby in the beginning, and it hadn't lasted. And Sofia loved Niko too much to end up in a relationship where they would one day end up hurting each other or, worse, hating each other. Niko deserved better than that. He was a great guy. Someday he'd find his forever girl. It…it just wasn't her.

As Sofia settled into the back of Niko's limo at JFK airport, her heart was heavy. Niko joined her, but he was absorbed in a phone conversation. The laughter. The teasing. The kisses. The whispered sweet nothings of the night before ceased to exist in the light of day. Everything they'd shared was like a dream now.

She couldn't even bring herself to meet Niko's gaze. She shouldn't have let things go so far last night. She'd let herself believe there was something lasting between them that never really existed, and it was now going to make their parting today so much harder.

In no time, their car eased into New York City traffic and headed toward her home. They only had mere minutes left together. She didn't know what to say, so she remained silent while Niko continued texting on his phone. She didn't have to ask; she knew he was working. Those couple of days without internet had really put him behind.

She should text Kyra and let her know she'd arrived in New York, but she didn't feel like it. Kyra would have questions, and Sofia didn't like the answers she would have to give her. She'd contact her later.

"Are you feeling all right?" Niko's voice interrupted her thoughts.

"Um...yes. Why?"

"You're just so quiet this morning. I was worried you might have morning sickness."

"No. I'm okay." *Liar. Liar.*

She did have an upset stomach, but it wasn't too bad. And right now it was difficult to tell if it was from the baby or from the thought of saying goodbye to Niko. Now that he'd revealed his gentle, caring side to her, he'd crept right past her defenses as though they weren't even there. If only—

"Just tell me if you need anything," he said.

Like getting away from you before you break my heart? But it was too late for that. Then she thought of the one thing they hadn't resolved on the trip—the raising of their child. "There is one thing."

"Name it." He sounded so formal, so distant this morning.

"It's the baby. We never set up any arrangements about raising him or her." She swallowed hard, clasped her hands together and tried to ignore the pounding of her heart in her ears. "I'd like it if you'd agree to let me raise the baby here in New York. My family is big and loud, but their hearts are bigger than the world. Once they know I'm pregnant, they'll be so excited about the baby, and I'll never have to worry about a babysitter." As Niko's frown deepened, she realized she'd failed to mention something important. "And you will always be welcome, as much as your schedule allows. I know how busy you are."

She just couldn't meet his gaze and risk him reading the pain and disappointment in her eyes. She turned to the window. She recognized their surroundings. Their time together was almost up. And yet Niko wouldn't respond. She had no idea what he was thinking, and it was making her increasingly uncomfortable.

She forced herself to face him. "Niko, please say something."

"I don't have an answer for you."

"Oh." She knew he had enough money to hire a whole army of nurses to care for the baby and provide opportunities for their child that she could never afford, but he seemed reasonable. Surely he wouldn't want a long, drawn-out court battle like those she'd read about in the paper.

He cleared his throat. "Why don't you come back to the penthouse with me? You could see the hotel."

No. She couldn't. It'd be too easy for him to try to sway her with his mesmerizing blue-gray eyes or with his lopsided smile. Or worse, a kiss or two. She was already so confused. She didn't need to further complicate matters.

"I'm sorry but my parents are expecting me." It wasn't a lie. She'd called them from the airport. Her mother was probably already cooking pasta with meatballs as well as calling Sofia's aunts and cousins. Her mother's side of the family was enormous.

"You're sure?" When she nodded, not trusting herself to speak, he said, "Okay."

She wasn't sure. Not sure about anything.

Just stay busy.

That was what Niko had been telling himself all morning. If he stayed busy enough, it wouldn't bother him when Sofia left. And she certainly seemed anxious enough to get away from him today. He glanced down at the gaping space between them.

How could things have changed so drastically in the light of day? It was as if they were back to being those two awkward people that had run into each other in his bungalow back at the Blue Tide Resort. And he hated that they were going backward in their relationship after how much progress they'd made.

He glanced at her as she gazed at the bustling city around them. For a moment, he considered proposing again, but she'd been so quiet and distant all day. She regretted their lovemaking. That must be it.

Yet, last night he'd been so sure that she'd been enjoying the closeness as much as him. Frustration churned in his gut. What was he missing?

Unable to figure out where things had gone astray with Sofia, he turned his thoughts to something he could control: the sale of the Stravos Star Hotel in Manhattan. It had always been his favorite. Maybe it was being in this particular city. It practically vibrated with energy. It'd be a shame to sell it.

He cleared his throat. "I'm thinking of keeping the hotel here in the city."

"But I thought you had an agreement with Cristo to sell all of them."

"We're still in negotiations. And Cristo already has a hotel here." And then he realized that Sofia already knew this. "The one where you work."

"Why would you keep it when you're selling all of the rest? I thought you planned to consolidate your assets into the shipping business."

He shrugged. "I can afford this indulgence. And since I'll be spending a lot of time in New York, it'll come in handy."

"You'll be here often?"

Why did she have to sound so surprised? Did she really think he'd end up like his grandfather, sequestered on that island with nothing but his work for company? He refused to let that be his future. "Yes. I'll be commuting between Greece and the States. I plan to expand the shipping business to the States."

"Oh. I didn't know."

Before Niko could tell her his main reason for coming back would be for her and the baby, the limo pulled to a stop in front of a townhome. It was well kept with potted plants lining the steps up to the black door with gold numbers. Suddenly the front door swung open, and smiling people rushed forth. Sofia's big, loud, loving family.

Unwilling to lose her, he uttered, "Sofia, come back to the hotel with me. We can make this work."

She shook her head and blinked repeatedly. "It won't work."

"Why not? We've learned so much about each other on this trip. If it's my business—"

"It's not. Not really."

"Then what is it?"

Sofia's gaze moved past him to the crowd forming on the sidewalk before returning to him. "Do you love me?"

His mouth opened, but no words came out. He wanted to tell her what she wanted to hear, but the truth was he didn't know. How was he supposed to know what love was when he'd never experienced it? Not really. Sure, he loved his grandfather, but that had been a very complicated dynamic. His grandfather had never been an easy man to get close to.

Niko had never been in love. He'd never allowed himself to go there. He did feel something for Sofia. He just didn't know how to put it into words.

When the silence dragged on, Sofia said, "That's what I thought. It'll be better for everyone, including the baby, if we end whatever it was here and now while we're still friends."

Her door swung open, and she stepped out, engulfed in hugs by a sea of smiling, laughing, talking-all-at-once people. So this was what it was like to be part of a large family. *Interesting.*

Niko wasn't about to leave. Not yet. He wanted to meet Sofia's family. She frowned at him as he exited the limo and moved to her side, but he pretended not to notice. He wanted to meet the people that would have such a big influence on his son or daughter.

An older woman with a bit of gray streaking through her dark hair eyed him. "Sofia, who's your friend?"

"Mama, this is Niko, erm, Mr. Stravos."

"Oh, he's the one you've been working for?"

Color tinged Sofia's cheeks as she nodded.

So that's what she'd told her family. He had wondered about that. And he was guessing they still didn't know about the baby. That would be one conversation he'd like to be a part of.

Realizing that his manners were lacking, he held out his hand to her mother. Sofia's mother took his hand and pulled him close. She hugged him. It was not a greeting he was accustomed to in his world.

When Sofia's mother pulled back, she sent him a knowing smile. So she didn't buy her daughter's story, after all. "It's nice to meet you, Mr. Stravos."

"Please call me Niko."

"And call me Maria."

An older man worked through the crowd on the sidewalk, calling out to Sofia's mother. It had to be Sofia's father. Niko steeled himself for a protective father. Niko would be the same way if he had a daughter as beautiful as Sofia. But someone stepped in front of her father, engaging him in conversation.

Sofia leaned over and whispered, "You don't belong here. Please go."

As he looked around at her loving family, he realized she had everything she needed right here. And he had nothing to offer her—not the epic love she deserved. Sofia should have a man who knew how to cook her an elaborate dinner and knew all the details of her life, big and small. Like the fact that she was allergic to flowers.

The weight of failure mingled with guilt pressed down on his shoulders. He didn't know how to turn his back on a future with Sofia, but he didn't see any other choice. He would contact her later about custody arrangements. At least they were still on friendly terms.

He leaned close to her, taking in one last whiff of her honeyed scent. "This isn't over. We will talk."

Her eyes widened, but she didn't say anything.

He'd meant they would talk about their child, but as he made his excuses to her mother, he wondered if Sofia had misunderstood. He should correct her, but he couldn't bring himself to do it. He couldn't admit that he wasn't the man for her. He climbed in the limo, never having felt more alone in his life.

CHAPTER TWENTY-ONE

WHAT HAD SHE DONE?

Sofia paced back and forth in her childhood bedroom. She hadn't been able to keep her dinner down. There was no lying to her mother, not that she'd planned to, but her mother was sometimes just too astute. She'd figured out Sofia was pregnant and that Niko was the father.

What her mother couldn't understand was why Sofia had turned him away. When Sofia attempted to explain her reasoning, the words didn't sound as convincing as they had in the limo. Had she made the biggest mistake of her life?

A knock at the bedroom door made her pause. She didn't want to talk to anyone. She felt physically exhausted and emotionally raw.

Without waiting for a response, her mother walked in. "Here." She held out a glass of what looked to be ginger ale on ice. "These saltines should help settle your stomach."

"Thanks, Mom."

"You know, I was sick my entire pregnancy with you. Might be one of the reasons you were the last. But no worries. This too shall pass."

"I don't think it's the baby." It was her own mess that was weighing on her.

"What's bothering you?" Her mother sat on the edge of the twin bed with the purple comforter that had been all the rage when Sofia was a teenager.

"Everything."

"That's a lot of stuff. No wonder you're not feeling well."

That was one thing she liked about her mother, she wasn't quick to solve her children's problems. She let each of them solve them for themselves and only stepped in when necessary. Her theory was that kids had to learn to stand on their own feet at some point. Only right now Sofia could definitely use some advice.

"I think I love him." Sofia's voice was soft, as she'd never admitted those words aloud.

"You think? You don't know?"

"Okay. Yes. I love Niko."

"So then what are you doing moping here in your old bedroom instead of being with him?"

"He…he doesn't love me." The pain of the admission pierced her heart. She moved to her window, which looked out over the quiet street, not ready to face her mother yet.

"Oh." There was a distinct pause as though her mother was digesting this information. "I take it he told you this?"

Sofia shook her head. "No. The problem is he wouldn't say the words."

"You, um, asked him?"

"Uh-huh." She sniffled, holding back a new wave of disappointment. "I thought he did. I really did."

"You always were quick to jump to conclusions as a kid—"

"But I didn't. Or at least I didn't think I had." She searched back over her memories of her time with Niko. All the signs were there that he loved her. Weren't they?

"So which is it?"

Sofia turned to face her mother. "I…I don't know. He took such good care of me after they released me from the hospital—"

"What hospital?" Her mother jumped to her feet. "What's wrong? Why didn't you call?"

Oops! She hadn't meant to let that part slip. She knew how her mother worried over her. So Sofia started at the beginning of the whole story, including Niko's journey to find the pictures and letters from his family.

"I'm so relieved you and the baby are okay." Her mother moved to the door, about to leave. "You know, Sofia, you've been dealt a bad hand when it comes to love, but you can't judge all men based on Bobby. And for the part I played in that disaster, I apologize. I learned my lesson about sticking my nose in where it doesn't belong."

"It's okay. You didn't do anything but get excited about my engagement. I wouldn't have wanted anything different. I never blamed you for any of it."

"Thank you." Her mother hesitated as though trying to decide if she should stay or go. "You know, some men can say all of the right things and not mean any of them. Other men struggle with the words but do all of the right things."

Her mother slipped out the door, leaving Sofia alone with her thoughts. Why couldn't she have one of those mothers who told her kids what to do? It would be so much easier.

Sofia knew what she wanted to do, but was it the right thing? Her hands moved to her expanding midsection. There was more than just herself to consider now.

CHAPTER TWENTY-TWO

UNABLE TO SLEEP, Niko skulked through the penthouse.

He'd never felt so profoundly alone. Being with Sofia had shown him what it was like to be part of a team—to have someone to lean on and to talk to. Now the silence was deafening.

How could he have let her get away? Why couldn't he just tell her what she wanted to hear? That he loved her.

Because he honestly didn't know how to describe these feelings he had for her. They were so strong at times that they scared him. He'd never felt this way before. Was it real? Or was it infatuation? How was he supposed to know the difference? He just couldn't mess this up. He had to be certain.

He turned on the desk lamp in the study and sat down at the desk. If he wasn't going to sleep, at least he could get some work done. He turned his laptop on. That would help. He'd be able to center his thoughts on his shipping business—a project that would mark his name on the world.

His fingers moved over the keyboard, but he soon found it wasn't business that kept him typing. Instead he was researching business schools, wondering which ones Sofia would apply to. And then he started searching for information about babies. It was amazing how much information was online. There were even pictures of how the baby might look at this stage. The breath caught in his throat. He was going to miss out on so much.

He clenched his hands and groaned in frustration. How was it that he could lead one of the world's biggest companies and make million-dollar decisions that would affect many lives and yet he didn't know how to deal with the emotional land mines of being a family man?

In that moment he realized he wanted to learn to be the man Sofia and their baby could count on. He wanted that more than running the Stravos Trust and more than heading up his shipping business. He wanted to be a part of Sofia's life now and forever.

And then he realized why he wanted to marry Sofia, and it had nothing to do with obligations or that it was the right thing to do. And it wasn't even the little baby she was carrying. She was his family. It was her—Sofia was his home. Plain and simple.

He loved her.

At first the admission scared him. The more he thought about it, the less scary the concept became. He, Niko Stravos, loved Sofia Moore. He smiled. Why did he have to make something so simple into something so complicated?

Now he had to prove his love to her. Would words be enough? Or was it too late? No, he couldn't believe that.

Wishing there was someone he could go to for advice, he wondered if his grandfather had left him anything in the penthouse like he had at the other stops on the trip. Niko headed straight for the floor safe in the bedroom closet. Inside he found an envelope with his name on it. The bold letters were in his grandfather's handwriting.

The last letter his grandfather had written him had sent him on the journey of his life. Something told him this letter was going to affect him just as profoundly, but he had no idea in what way.

Niko moved to sit on the bed. His finger slipped through the opening at the edge of the envelope.

He ripped it open, anxious to find out what his grandfather had to impart to him this time.

Niko,

By now you have completed the journey I have set out for you. I hope you were able to appreciate your heritage in a way that I never shared with you. I am sorry I wasn't able to open up about the past. I made too many mistakes and had too many regrets.

Learn from my errors. Don't get so obsessed with the company that you forsake those you care most for in life. The lesson I learned too late was that in the end, love is what counts. It's the important total on life's balance sheet. Don't let it pass you by.

It won't be easy. Nothing in life worth having will come to you easily. Don't give up. If it's important enough, stick with it.

Don't end up old and alone. The company is no substitute for an amazing woman by your side.

I love you.

Immediately Sofia's face came to mind. And then an image of her holding their baby. Niko vowed then and there not to give up. Because as much as he loved his work, he loved her more.

And then Niko noticed a note scrawled at the bottom of the letter:

In the back of the safe is a small box. It is yours now. Make sure you put it to good use.

Intrigued, Niko rushed back to the safe. In the dark, he felt around until his fingers came in contact with the box. He pulled it out and surmised it was a ring box. There was a message attached.

This first belonged to your great-grandmother, then your grandmother and lastly your mother. It is now yours, for your bride. Take it and create your own happiness.

Niko opened the box, finding a beautiful diamond solitaire. It wasn't fancy, but there was something appealing in its simplicity. And it would look perfect on Sofia's hand. He snapped the box shut.

Tomorrow he'd beg her to forgive him for being so slow with figuring out the truth—he loved her with all his heart. He sat back on the bed, opening the ring box again.

There was no way he was going to fall asleep. Not now. He was too anxious. Too worried. What if Sofia rejected him again? But what if she didn't?

He glanced at the clock. It was after midnight. Much too late to go pounding on Sofia's parents' door. But this couldn't wait. Surely they'd understand. He had to seize the moment—

A knock sounded at his door. An insistent knock. A knock that went on and on.

What in the world?

CHAPTER TWENTY-THREE

SOFIA WASN'T LEAVING until she had her say.

She realized Niko had every right to turn her away, especially after how she'd shut him down not only on top of Diamond Head, but also in the limo. In truth, she realized she didn't deserve another chance, but she had to try.

Her clenched hand continued to pound on the door. *Please let him be here.*

At last the door swung open.

"What the h—"

The words stopped as Niko's narrowed gaze settled on her. Immediately his tense stance eased. That had to be a good sign, right? She couldn't resist taking a second to appreciate that the only thing he was wearing was a pair of wine-colored boxers. She did seem to have perfect timing where he was concerned.

When her gaze returned to his face, she noticed that his hair was mussed up. "Did I wake you?"

"No. Come in. We need to talk."

So he couldn't sleep, either. *Interesting.* She stepped past him, careful not to touch him. She was already nervous enough.

"Sofia, listen I—"

She turned to him and placed a finger on his lips—his very tempting lips. So much for keeping a safe distance. A tingling sensation rushed up her arm and settled in her chest. Her heart pounded so loudly that it was hard to hear her own thoughts.

"I need to say this." She pulled her hand back. "Just listen." When he nodded, she continued, "I'm sorry." Her gaze met his. "I didn't realize it, but I was so afraid of you hurting me that I didn't see what was right in front of my eyes. I love you—"

Niko swept her up in his arms and pressed his lips to hers in a needy, hungry kiss. She didn't fight him, forgetting her speech. This said so much. It soothed her worries that he would turn her away. There was passion and undeniable need in his kiss. They'd figure out the rest as they went along.

Tangled limbs. Endless kisses. Pounding hearts. This was where she belonged. She knew it in her heart. And at last, Niko knew it, too. He was showing her in every loving touch.

Niko was the first to pull away. His forehead rested against hers as he drew in one unsteady breath after the other.

"I need to tell you something, too." Niko continued to hold on to her as though afraid if he let go, she'd disappear like a dream.

"I'm listening."

"I was just about to head out the door and go to your parents' house."

"Well, that would have been quite a scene."

"Because it's so late?"

"No, because of your lack of clothes." She tugged on the waistband of his boxers.

"You're so funny."

"I try."

"And that's one of the reasons I love you."

"What?" This time Sofia did pull away. She had to be sure of what she'd heard. "Say that again."

"I love you, Sofia Moore. I love the way you smile. I love the way you care for others. I love everything about you. And I'm sorry it took me so long to figure it out."

"You…you mean it?" When he nodded, she added, "And you're not just saying this because you know it's what I want to hear?"

"I would never do that. This is too important.

If we're going to make it through the years like your parents, it has to be genuine."

Tears of happiness sprang to her eyes and she blinked repeatedly. "I love you, too." Then she took Niko's hand and placed it on her tiny baby bump. "Did you hear that, baby? We're home for always and forever."

EPILOGUE

Four months later, Athens, Greece...

"DID YOU EVER see such handsomeness?"

A smile tugged at Niko's lips as he listened to the nurses whisper back and forth. He was used to the attention, but he didn't want their admiration to bother his wife after she'd worked so hard to bring their son into this world.

Their son.

The words still sounded so unreal to his ears. He was now a father. He sat on the edge of his wife's hospital bed, holding her hand. Her eyes were closed as she rested while they cleaned up the baby.

"He really is handsome," came another female voice.

He'd have to put a stop to this before Sofia heard it. After all, he was a happily married man now. He didn't have time for flirting, no matter how cute the nurse. He only had eyes for one lady, and she was lying next to him. She'd opened up a whole new world to him.

Niko slipped off the bed, trying not to disturb his wife. He turned to the women as they continued to whisper more compliments. In truth, he was extremely flattered, but he just couldn't let it go on.

"Excuse me." He stepped closer to the cluster of nurses.

The women moved apart and turned to him with smiles on their faces. His gaze landed on his son in one of the nurse's arms. Realization dawned on him. They were oohing and aahing over Ari.

"Would you like to hold your son?" The nurse approached him. "He's so darling."

"Um...yes. Thank you." Embarrassment hit him like a brick wall. He was starting to realize he was no longer in the forefront of people's attention—from this point forward his son would be the shining Stravos star.

And that was totally fine with Niko. He never knew having a wife and a baby could feel this good. Being a family man meant more to him than buying his first megacargo carrier, which he'd just christened that week the *STC Ari*, named after his son, Nikolas Ari Stravos IV.

"Niko, bring him closer." Sofia's voice was anxious.

He moved swiftly to her side, and, knowing exactly what was needed, he eased Ari into his mother's arms. Nothing had ever looked so good.

"He looks just like his father." Sofia smiled up at him.

"You think so?" Niko glanced down at his handsome son. He didn't know how much he resembled him, but if his wife said so, that was good enough for him. "He looks happy."

"Of course he is—he's with his mom and dad." Sofia ran her finger over their son's chubby cheek.

Niko was awed by the immediate bond between mother and son. "Are you sure you'll be able to part with him now that you've been accepted into the university?"

"I don't have classes for a few more months." She continued to smile and make cooing noises.

He knew Sofia followed through on things, but he also knew separating mother from son, even for a few hours a day, would not be easy. Even he didn't know how he'd go back to the office and leave both of them. He was already planning to work from home as much as possible. Their trip around the world had taught him many things, including how to work remotely.

Niko cleared his throat. "Not to ruin this moment, but are you ready to see the godparents? I think you made them a little nervous when you went into labor a month early."

"They were nervous? How about you?" Her accusing stare landed on him.

"What? I wasn't worried at all. I knew you had everything under control." *Yeah, right.* He'd never been so scared in his life. He'd had no idea what to say or what to do, but somehow Sofia seemed to keep it all together as if it was all natural to her.

"Well, then that makes one of us because I was really worried. I've never had a baby before, let alone delivered a month early and in a different country from the one we were planning. You know my family is going to be really upset about this. We were supposed to deliver Ari in New York."

Niko hadn't thought about that. When Sofia said she had a big family, she hadn't been kidding. He could barely keep her brothers' names straight, and when it came to her cousins he was at an utter loss. There had to be at least twenty—no, make that thirty—of them.

"Let me get Kyra and Cristo."

In no time, he was ushering his cousin and her husband into the private hospital room. Niko took his rightful position next to his wife and son. Nothing had ever felt so right. "Say hello to your godchild."

"Really? You want us to be his godparents?" As Niko and Sofia nodded, Kyra's eyes glistened with unshed tears. "Aww...thank you."

Cristo held out his hand. Niko shook his hand before pulling him into a hug. He was just so darn happy and proud of his family. The men quickly pulled apart just as Kyra scooped Ari up in her arms. She immediately placed a kiss atop his head. That boy was going to have all the women wrapped around his finger in no time.

Kyra's gaze moved from the baby to her husband. "Maybe you're right."

"Right about what?" Sofia sat up in bed, her face aglow with curiosity.

Color bloomed in Kyra's cheeks. "Cristo thinks we should start a family, but I wasn't so sure. But now after holding little Ari, I'm starting to think he might be right."

"That would be great." Sofia smiled. "Our kids can grow up together."

"They'll be the best of friends. Just like us."

"Yes, just like us."

Niko couldn't think of anything he'd like better. His family was expanding in ways he'd never thought of, and yet it was growing closer. And he couldn't be happier.

As Kyra and Cristo fussed over the baby, Niko leaned over to his wife and whispered, "I love you."

She glanced up at him. "I love you, too."

* * * * *

In case you missed it,
Book One in Jennifer Faye's
BRIDES FOR THE GREEK TYCOONS *duet,*
THE GREEK'S READY-MADE WIFE,
is available now!